OUT OF NOWHERE

A MELANIE KROUPA BOOK

Books by Ouida Sebestyen

OUT OF NOWHERE

A NOVEL BY

OUIDA SEBESTYEN

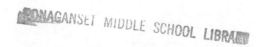

ORCHARD BOOKS
NEW YORK

Orchard Books
95 Madison Avenue
New York, NY 10016

Manufactured in the United States of America
The text of this book is set in 12 point Garamond No. 3.
Book design by Sylvia Frezzolini

10   9   8   7   6   5   4   3   2   1

Library of Congress Cataloging-in-Publication Data
Sebestyen, Ouida.   Out of nowhere : a novel / by Ouida Sebestyen.
p.   cm.   "A Melanie Kroupa book"—Half t.p.
Summary: When he no longer fits into his vagabond mother's life, thirteen-year-old Harley
adopts an abandoned dog and falls in with an outspoken old woman, a cantankerous junk
collector, and an energetic and loving teenage girl.
ISBN 0-531-06839-0.   ISBN 0-531-08689-5 (lib. bdg.)
[1. Dogs—Fiction.   2. Foster home care—Fiction.]   I. Title.
PZ7.S4440u   1994   93-37759
[Fic]—dc20

To Jerry and Peggy

and the others

ONE

Oh, God, I hate this, Harley thought, following Vernie out of the bait store. She should've known it's not going to work.

They got into the waiting BMW. "I can't believe this," Vernie said to the man tapping the steering wheel impatiently. She sounded shocked. "The people in there said Daddy's dead. Just a few days ago. He was parked up on that little hill, and somebody came by his RV and found him. Could we just—go up there for a minute? We can't pay our last respects sitting here."

The man stared at her in silence. His rings clicked on the steering wheel as he decided. All at once he started the Bimmer and swung it around into the gravel road Vernie was pointing to. Harley hunched tight in the backseat as the thorny bushes flashed by. Maybe she was going to pull it off after all.

From out of nowhere, it seemed, they were overtaken and passed by a pickup with no muffler. Its radio blared a moment and faded. Harley saw a black-and-white dog staring at them from the truck bed as it disappeared in a glow of dust.

At the top of the hill, the man veered off the road and pulled up beside a table in a picnic area. Harley sat up

1

straight. A long, unexpected lake lay in a hollow of the desert below them.

Vernie looked around. "I bet he was parked right here. Waiting for us to come." She turned to Harley. "You were all set to stay up here with Daddy in his big old motor thing, weren't you, babe?" She gazed out again, sadly. "I guess somebody's already taken it away. Sold to pay for the funeral, maybe. This is such a shock. I still can't believe it."

The man glanced at his show-off watch, and then at the sun getting low in the west. "Neither can I, Vernie. I think you're lying. I think you've made up this whole cockeyed story."

"You what?" Harley tried not to cringe as Vernie's voice skidded up in her best imitation of astonishment. "I've got Daddy's *letter* here someplace, for God's sake. Inviting Harley. Can I help it if he *died?*"

She grabbed up her purse and raked around in it. Harley longed to peel himself off the leather seat and slide out into clean air. With one corner of his mind, he realized that the lake was as fake as what they were doing—held there, where it didn't belong, by a dam. The bony branches of drowned trees stuck up out of it.

Vernie said, "Everybody there at the store had heard about it. It happened really suddenly—didn't they say a heart attack, Harley? They were all talking at once."

Harley cleared his throat and murmured, "Yeah—heart attack," certain that the man knew he was lying right along with Vernie.

2

She triumphantly drew a snapshot out of her purse. "Here! Here's Harley and Daddy, back when Daddy lived in the garage apartment behind us, down on the beach. We've known him since Harley was *five*, for God's sake."

Memories rushed at Harley as Vernie shoved the picture at the man. It hurt that she was using Daddy and his death in her little act.

The man pushed her hand away. "You're overplaying it, Vernie. I don't care how many Daddys you come up with—we need to get one thing straight right now, okay? This is as far as the kid goes."

Harley felt all his clutched feelings drop away like groceries from a wet sack.

"You've got to be joking!" she protested. "He's thirteen years old, for God's sake, and it's about to get dark."

The man said, "So? When I was his age, I was pulling down more money than my old man. Look, I've brought him this far because you said there was somebody out here you were going to leave him with. Now you're saying there's not anybody. *I'm* just saying here's where he gets out."

Harley held his breath as they had a staring match. He wanted to yell at her, Why didn't you pretend Daddy was waiting someplace closer to Houston, so by then this guy would've just taken me the rest of the way? You've sprung everything too fast, and ruined it!

The man said, "I don't need a third wheel, Vernie. I'm paying *your* expenses—that's all—so stop trying to pad our deal with stunts like this."

3

Vernie suddenly made a little laugh that sounded scared. "Hey. No problem." She shrugged. "He can go back."

Harley felt his muscles bunch up in disbelief. He watched as the man stretched his arm along the back of Vernie's seat and trailed one finger along the edge of her orange tank top, murmuring, "Right." His eyes unexpectedly met Harley's in the rearview mirror.

With sudden cold calmness, Harley turned to look out at the lake. Its stillness was almost a shock. He needed the shoving restless ocean to match his feelings, not tiny people fishing along an inlet with their RVs parked in the brush just like the one Vernie had made up for Daddy. It unnerved him to think he had never been this far away from traffic and buildings and lights before, with night coming. How could she have said it so easily? With a little laugh. *He can go back.*

An aching sadness he had known before flooded over him, carrying all the loneliness and ruined hopes of his life like silt. As it grew, he began to take the hard, deep breaths he always took at track meets just before his turn to run.

The man said abruptly, "Okay, stick him on a bus, the next town we get to. I'll buy him a ticket back home. Are you satisfied? Now I'm going to take a leak." He got out of the car and walked off.

Harley unclinched himself and got out, too, gulping the warm, dry air. He was startled to see a gray-haired woman spreading out her supper on another picnic table only a few yards away behind some scrubby trees.

Vernie's still-taut face poked through the window, smiling. "Hey, that worked out pretty good, babe—a free ticket."

"Back *home*!" he said, amazed at her.

"Hey, I knocked myself out trying to get him to let you come. He's just not going to do it, Harley."

"Argue with him," he protested. "There's no home for me to go back to. Remember? Even the little guy in L.A. can't keep us anymore. Isn't that why we're doing *this*?"

"We're doing this because it's too good not to grab. He's got connections with entertainment people like you wouldn't believe. He says I'll—"

"No, I wouldn't believe," he agreed.

"I'll have all new costumes. And publicity—he's going to fix me up the way I've always dreamed about."

"You know how he'll fix you up," he said wearily.

She reached out and caught his arm. "Hey, listen to me. I'm going to *do* this. It's for you, too—and you might as well play along."

"Why?" he demanded. "Where?"

"Check with Pinkie when you get back to the coast. Remember her—where we used to eat? She'll know lots of places you can stay. Maybe you can even work at the café a little." Her eyes slid past him. "It'll really be better than hanging around Houston while I work. It really will be, or I wouldn't send you back." Her face, under its tired makeup, suddenly looked younger than it was. "God, tonight when it's my turn to drive and he's asleep, I'm going to—to just *blaze* across that desert, a hundred and ten miles an hour." Both her hands gave the leather seat a caress. "Don't you *love* this gorgeous car?"

He almost said, Not really, but I guess I could sure use any love you've got left over. But the gray-haired woman was still at the next picnic table, holding something she had forgotten to eat as she stared across the water. She didn't have a camper, just an old station wagon with a thermos jug on the let-down tailgate. He guessed she'd already heard an earful.

He said, "I don't want to go back."

"Oh, sure you do, babe. With a free ticket—and maybe even dinner if you have to wait long. It's going to work out really good out there. You already know some kids, and where school is—"

The man came out of the privy at the edge of the campground and started toward them. Before Harley could stop himself he said, "Tell him you won't come if I can't come."

She looked at him in silence. Were her eyes a little sad? He tried to see regret. But all he could see was tiredness. Conning was hard work, even when she was doing it to herself.

He turned away and stared at three tall old cactuses growing beside the road with their arms lifted as if their stagecoach had been held up. He had no idea what to do now. God, he thought, I need some help here.

As he stood frozen in uncertainty, he heard the pickup that had passed them earlier. It must have turned around somewhere up the road, because he suddenly glimpsed it coming back in a glow of dust, the only thing moving in the clear, eerie twilight.

He began to walk toward the little bluff that dropped off to the lake, picking his way around the rocks. As he passed the old woman, her gaze moved from the water to his face, and for a second, her sharp, squinty eyes locked with his.

He wondered how good her hearing was. He stumbled over a rock and angled off from her as the sadness in him shifted like something permanently loose and dangerous in his head.

The pickup sped past in a squawk of music. As he turned to look, a beer can flew out of the cab. Then the black-and-white dog he had seen in the back earlier came tearing along behind it, sending up its own little spurts of dust. He watched as it flung itself down the road, straining to catch up as the distance between it and the truck got wider and wider. It passed a patch of brush and was out of sight, then reappeared, smaller, a galloping black bug.

Harley stopped short, realizing he had moved forward as he watched, mesmerized, and was about to bump into the Bimmer. Vernie and the man were watching, too, inside, and Vernie said, "Hey, jerks, you forgot your pooch."

The pickup disappeared over a ridge. In a moment the dog came into view again, still running its heart out in a race it had already lost.

"Looks like they've ditched him," the man said, turning away.

"Can they do that?" Harley asked, startled. Wasn't there some kind of law that you couldn't just get rid of whatever you didn't want around anymore?

"They just did," Vernie said. "He's dumped and don't know it—happens to the best of us."

The man glanced at her, almost smiling. "Looks like he don't take no for an answer any better than you do."

Vernie lifted the hot hair off her neck. "At least go down slugging, I always say." She smiled back and let her hand drop to rest on the man's thigh. "Harley," she called, "hop in. We're invited to dinner."

Harley bit his chapped lip and stared straight ahead. "Go yourself," he told her. "I don't want dinner."

Vernie blew out her breath. "Okay—what are you trying to pull?"

"Nothing." He swallowed hard to wet his dry mouth. "Not a thing. I'm just not hopping in, that's all. I'd rather stay here." He could feel his skin flushing hot. I know I've got to do this, he thought. Finally got to do it. Right now.

The man said, "Hey, let's go."

"Well, start the engine!" Vernie ordered. "Harley, get in the damn car."

"Why should I?" He was seized by the quick, protective anger that made people yell, Hey, you can't fire me—I quit! He put his hands on the edge of Vernie's window and looked in at the man. "I don't want your dinner or your bus fare or your leather seats or anything else you have. I don't like you."

Through the pounding in his head, he heard the man make what sounded like a little surprised grunt of amusement.

Vernie said, "Shut up, Harley."

He turned to her. "I don't like you, either. Or your lying and mooching and drifting around and promising us a house." It was coming out for the first time ever, like a blast from a fire hose he couldn't turn off. "I don't like how it is. Living with you. Or what I'm turning out to be, or how to change it—"

Vernie reached out and grabbed his shirtfront. Her eyes were fiery. "What you're turning out to be is a little smart-ass. Was I supposed to change my whole life just because you dropped out of nowhere and started cluttering it up?"

"Yes," he gasped.

"Well, forget *that*!" She gave him a jerk. "You've been one big, long burden, Harley—ruining my opportunities right and left for thirteen years. It's time for me to get on with my life, for God's sake."

The man groaned in annoyance and started the Bimmer.

Harley broke Vernie's grip on his shirt and stepped out of reach. He looked around, dazed, as if he had just rammed through a wall in his life and was somewhere he had never been before. He said evenly, "I want my duffel. Unlock the trunk. I want my clothes."

He walked to the back of the Bimmer and let his fist come down hard on the lid. That got results. When he felt the click that unlocked the trunk from inside, he pulled his lumpy duffel bag out from under Vernie's pile of luggage.

Vernie yelled, "Harley, he's trying to give you a free ride. What's the matter with you?"

Harley slammed the trunk lid down. He was too numb to wonder yet what he'd done. Or be sorry for his outburst or shocked at Vernie's. He began to back away. He wanted them to get smaller and smaller till they were specks in one of those long, receding camera shots at the end of movies.

Vernie called from the window, "Don't you know this is stupid? You can't get a ride to L.A. from out here. Why can't you be reasonable?"

He was still backing off when he felt himself go over the edge of the little bluff. He flung his arms out like an idiot and toppled down a slope in a clattering rush of rubble. Something thorny caught his duffel, and he snatched at its branches, still sliding. Twigs flicked across his cheek and ear as he jolted to a stop against a rock.

"Harley?" Vernie called again. He stood up into view, glad he had been out of sight when he fell, and dusted the seat of his jeans. "Okay, you asked for this," she reminded him. "I got you a good deal, and you turned your back on it. Just remember that."

He stepped out of her sight again. He could hear the Bimmer's tires crunch stones as it circled.

Vernie yelled at the man, "Hey! You started this whole thing—you can at least leave him some money!" He heard the car stop, and then move on. "Harley," she called, "look in the road. Get on back to the coast whatever smart-ass way you want to. Ask at the café. I'll let Pinkie know where I am. She'll get you set up good." Her voice had gradually gotten smaller—crushed, too, beneath the noise of the car, until it drifted back to him like dust.

He turned around and looked at the lake a long time, brushing at the twigs stuck in his shirt. He guessed he was listening for a we-thought-it-over-and-are-turning-around sound, but finally there was no sound at all.

He climbed back up the slope. He could see the car dimly in the distance. It didn't blaze. It looked like one of those miniatures in hobby shops as it wound through the desert brush on its glinty button wheels. Suddenly it disappeared over the ridge the way the pickup and the dog had.

"Varoom," he said softly to it. "Va-room." He walked back to the spot where it had been parked and picked up a twenty-dollar bill.

TWO

The gray-haired woman who had been at the picnic table took a few steps toward Harley and pointed. "Under that big bush," she said. "Something blew over there when the car started off."

He went where she pointed and scuffed the weeds with his foot. For some reason he couldn't let himself stoop down and hunt as if it mattered.

"No," she said. "Farther over." She came closer and pointed out another twenty. He folded it with the first one and put them in his pocket.

"Well, big deal," he said brightly, wishing she'd butt out and leave him alone. "Money from heaven."

"Manna. But the modern equivalent, I guess." Up close she was kind of old, and saggy in places, with a prim face and wispy hair. "Maybe there's more," she said, poking the weeds.

"Don't bet on it." Forty was better than he had expected.

"That won't get you far."

He looked at the road the car had taken. "It's plenty for food, if I hitchhike."

She sized him up. "Good Lord," she said. "Please. Don't hitchhike back."

"Who said anything about going back?" he asked, turning on her. "I'm not about to go back."

"Well, pardon *me*." She looked startled. "What *are* you about to do? Roost in a saguaro tonight?"

He kicked up something that turned out to be a candy wrapper. It was all he could do to keep from warning her, Back off, lady—you're crowding me. But he said, "That's those big huge cactuses with the arms? I've slept in worse places."

"I don't doubt it." She drew a deep breath. "Well, get over here first, and let me wash the blood off your face."

He felt his ear and cheek. They were sticky. "Jeez, am I bleeding?"

"Well, it's customary to, when you make a slit in yourself." She went back to her picnic spot and saturated a paper napkin with what looked like iced tea from her thermos. He got his duffel and followed.

She didn't *plip-plip* away at his face the way women cleaned the heroes' faces in the movies. She scrubbed the cold, wet napkin across his cheek and down the side of his neck, stopping to fold it inside out when it began to turn pink.

"What did I do to myself?" he asked, wishing he had a mirror. His cheek burned. He tried to touch it again, but she nudged his hand away.

"You let yourself get left in the middle of Arizona with forty dollars and a change of socks."

"No—I mean—"

"I know what you mean. You're all right. Just leave it alone."

"It hurts," he muttered, feeling like a baby. He wasn't

used to people touching him. He wiped some drops that had gathered under his chin.

"Do you like tea?" she asked, pushing the thermos toward him.

"I guess not." He took an uncertain step backward. "I guess I'd better . . ." He started off with his duffel, and then turned around and came back. He didn't know what he'd better do. "Yeah," he said. "I like tea."

She poured him a lidful, and studied what she could see of his face as he drank. "I didn't think they'd leave you like that. Did you?"

He thought about it, staring over the lid. "I knew he wanted me out of the picture. From the start. But . . . I didn't know she did till right at the last there." He tried to work his way through the thumping confusion in his head. Maybe she had planned it to work out this way, and *he* was the only one she had conned.

"Well, what are you going to do? Ask somebody down there at the lake if you can sleep under their Winnebago?" She waited, tucking her head forward as if he might say something she would miss. "Think, Harley. It's getting dark."

He was too surprised at hearing his name to do anything but stare.

"It is Harley, isn't it?" she asked.

"Yeah." That settled whether her hearing was shot. It didn't seem to bother her to admit being nosy.

"She mentioned someone called Daddy," she said. "Was that your father? Your grandfather? Who died?"

He forgot and swiped at his cheek again, trying to think how much she could have heard. Not just the yelling parts, he guessed.

"I'm sorry he died," she said.

He wished she hadn't been taken in by Vernie's little act. But at least he could be honest about his own feelings. "Yeah, so am I. I wish I could've been coming to stay with him. I used to stay with him a lot when we all lived down by the beach." He was saying it crazy. He hadn't even said what state or town. But she nodded, as if she knew exactly where.

"Before he moved to Arizona," she said, helping.

"Yeah." He closed his eyes on the lie and started over. "No. He never came to Arizona. He died out there on the coast. Two years ago."

A real pain clutched him, for that real death. It nearly took his breath to think what a difference it would make if Daddy was still out there in his grubby little place over the garage, to go back to.

"I miss him," he said.

The woman took a sandwich out of a box on the table. "Try this." She held it out.

He hesitated. He needed it, if it would go down past the tightness. "Is it all right?" he asked.

Her eyebrows rose. "What—I'm going to poison you?"

"No—I mean is it all you've got to eat?"

Her face went soft again. "No. I made a bunch. Eat."

He unwrapped it. It was pimento cheese. It made five bites that tasted miraculous there in the desert.

"Another one?" she asked.

He took it. The lake and the evening sky had become the same glowing gray. He caught himself trying to hear the familiar sound of surf.

"Well?" she asked.

Far off on the other shore, a dog barked. Harley froze. Then a dwarfed voice called it, and he realized it had been a little nervous kind of dog. Not the big broad-chested dog that had run after the pickup. He made himself relax, and listened for what else might be out there. Coyotes, maybe. Later in the night. He couldn't let her push him. He gestured toward the water. "Is your husband still down there fishing?"

She looked out, too, turning her caught-off-guard face away. "No." After a moment she said in a different voice, "Well—who knows? He was never a fisherman—but, why not? Not down there. But, yes. Let's say he's fishing."

Whoa, he thought, not understanding a word she'd said. She was pretty odd, but he guessed that she just didn't want to say she was out there alone.

She turned back to face him squarely. "So who can we call—or find to put you up until you work this out?"

He shrugged, gripped by the sadness again. He hoped she wouldn't stop talking, no matter how little sense she made. He needed somebody saying words to him while he sorted out what had happened.

"So what about your real father?" she asked.

"I don't know. About him. He's not . . ." Now he

was the one hedging, not wanting to give a straight answer. He gathered his confidence. He couldn't make it worse. "My mom said it was just easier if she named me after a motorcycle. She was into that then, with these three guys she liked."

That hadn't been so bad. The woman's face didn't change as she gave him cookies from a sack and took one for herself.

He made a little laugh of relief. "So my name's Harley Nunn. See, because she had to fill out some papers about me, and the clerk or whatever said, 'Name of father?' And she said, 'None,' and this girl wrote down N-U-N-N, so that's how I am in the records—Harley Nunn. My mom said it had a ring to it."

"Where's your mother now?" she asked.

He couldn't believe how dense she was. He tilted his head toward the spot where the Bimmer had been. "That was her."

The woman murmured, "Good Lord. I was afraid so." She gazed at the spot. "How could she drive off like that?"

He lifted his shoulders and eyebrows as an answer. "She's used to leaving me. When I was little, she'd set me somewhere and forget to come back. That's how I got to know Daddy. She locked the doors and forgot to come home one night, and about midnight he saw me sitting on the step. So he came out and asked if I liked pizza, and let me sleep on his couch." He made another half-laugh so she could tell it was meant to be funny. "One time she forgot me and went to Mazatlán. But after a while she remembered, and called Daddy, and he came and found me, still at the Laundromat, where she'd left me. And after that I just sort of stayed up at his apartment when my mom was gone."

"When was that first time?"

"When I was five, I guess."

"Good Lord," she said again.

"It was handy to be with him. Because I had to go to school after that," he explained. "She was dancing, then, anyway. Different places. She was this exotic dancer. Her name's Lavern. She was even up in Alaska awhile, making really good money. She was going to buy us a house, but she never did." The sadness jolted in his head again. "She'd always get in with some guy and start using junk again."

"Like this man she's with now?"

He shrugged. "She thinks he's going to give her this terrific job. He's supposed to own this club in Houston or something. That was what all this stupid stuff was about—she didn't know what to do with me, so she was trying to scam him into taking me along. But it didn't work. Or maybe this was how she wanted it to work." His stomach kept gently churning. He wished she would pass the cookie sack again, but she stood up and swept everything off the table into a box. He'd talked too much, he guessed, and irritated her. But she was the one asking all the questions.

Finally she said, "You don't have anywhere to go, do

you, Harley?" She gazed around, as if she hoped somebody from social services would magically appear. "Who do I give you to? I've driven four hundred miles nonstop, and I'm tired. I want to crawl into the back of the station wagon and rest so I can be on the road all day tomorrow. It seemed like the simplest thing in the world when I parked here. Except that all of a sudden you're standing there with a bloody face and your little sack of clothes."

"Hey," he said, startled by her outburst. "No problem. I'm on my way down the road."

"Oh? And of course I'll sleep just fine as soon as you're out of sight." She shoved the box into the station wagon and slammed the door. "I don't know what to do. It's common sense not to let strangers—not to let just anybody—" She spread her hands helplessly. "This is ridiculous. I'm afraid of you, Harley. I don't know you. Or anyone like you. I'm afraid to say, 'Crawl in—there's room—we'll decide in the morning what to do with you.' "

He nodded. "Yeah, I know. You can't trust just anybody."

She came closer and sat on the edge of the table. "Are you afraid of me, too?"

It was too soon to tell, so he said carefully, "Well, you could be a weirdo as easy as I could. You could be running away from an institution or something yourself."

She looked out at the lake, which was disappearing in the darkness. "In a way I am."

"See?" he told her. He waited, but she kept staring into the dark. Soft small lights had come on in the campers. He could hear the little, high dog barks again, like someone tapping something. *Erk. Erk. Erk.*

"I'm a weirdo running away from home," she agreed. "What used to be home."

"Okay," he said.

"My name is May. Like the month. I didn't like being Mae with an *e*, so a long time ago I changed it. I was in love with a man named Nolan Woods, and if I married him, I would be May Woods. When I said those words to myself, I could see a beautiful forest, with trees full of white blossoms and new-green leaves."

Now we're getting really strange, he thought. But he asked her, "Did you get to be?"

"Yes."

"That's good."

"Well, no. Not anymore. That's why I'm running away."

Before he could stop the image, the black-and-white dog bolted across his mind. "Yeah? Where to?"

She turned toward what he took to be northeast. "Past all this, and over the mountains," she said. "On the other side there's a house that I lived in when I was your age. I'm going back to live in it again."

"Great," he said, and waited.

"It's going to be beautiful. Early June is magic there."

"Yeah?" He could feel her waiting, too.

"But right now I've got to get some sleep," she said.

"Sure." He began to back away.

"Harley—there's a small store down the road. Surely someone there can help, or . . ." She lifted her shoulders in regret as he started off.

"Right," he said briskly. He knew the bait store. He and Vernie had stood in a corner, where the man waiting in the BMW couldn't see them, until she said, "Okay, babe, let's get back out there and make this little scheme work."

But it didn't.

THREE

Somewhere along the smoother gravel of the main road, Harley glanced up at the sky and nearly staggered backward. He had never seen so many fat, bright, closely packed stars before. Like salt down the front of Vernie's black velvet robe when they pigged out on popcorn, watching TV.

Actually he could see that part of the sky wasn't salted. A dark mass had blotted out the stars and was bulging slowly upward. A flutter of sheet lightning played inside it.

He wheeled in a full, uncertain circle, looking around. Every one of the faint camper lights had gone off. He was on his own.

"Okay. You know this had to happen," he whispered. "Sooner or later."

His movement as he started forward again turned off the grating sound of insects as if he had broken some kind of electric circuit. He could hear them start again behind him, at home in their familiar darkness.

A few minutes later, he stopped again and pulled his only long-sleeved shirt out of the duffel. He yanked it on over his T-shirt. He had a news flash for Vernie. When they were packing, she'd said, "We're going through a desert, dummy—deserts are hot." This one was so cold his bones were rattling.

Or maybe he was shivering because he had actually faced up to her after a whole lifetime of nodding *Okay, I guess* to everything that happened.

He moved on, knowing he'd get really cold if he didn't. It was hard to judge time, there in the silence. He was maybe an hour along into—what? Six or seven hours of darkness? More stars had disappeared behind the cloud bank, and it was belching more sheet lightning as it grew.

A small sign loomed out of the darkness. He peered hopefully at it. BOAT RAMP, 1 MILE. He sighed and slumped to the ground against the post, figuring it was one thing that wouldn't have thorns on it. The lightning changed to real flashes that lit up the sky.

He emptied the gravel out of his shoe. Thunder rumbled, and just as it stopped, a metallic clink caught his attention. He froze. Something heavy rattled behind him and crashed to the ground. He lunged to his feet in such a panic he pitched his shoe out into the dark.

There was complete silence. He inched forward, stepped on his shoe, and snatched it on, still staring in the direction of the crash. He groped for his duffel and slowly crept forward into what seemed to be another picnic area. He could make out a table with benches. Then a big trash barrel, on its side, in a dribble of bottles and cans.

He froze again. Had somebody fallen over it? An animal? He felt a gust of cool air cross his sweaty face. *Something* was there, still near, watching him. The lightning flashed, nearly overhead, capturing a brief close-up of the fallen barrel. He blinked. The black-and-white dog had been in the picture. It had stood in the gray bushes with its head lowered intently, staring straight at Harley.

"Oh, God," he whispered, afraid to move. He had never been around any dog bigger than the little flea roost Daddy had had once. And this was not some floppy mop that would drink out of your glass while your back was turned. This was the kind of dog you handed your arm to if it insisted.

The lightning flared again. The dog was gone. Harley turned carefully in a circle, clutching the duffel to his chest like a shield. A few drops of rain hit his face.

He cleared his throat. "Having supper?" he asked shakily, remembering from somewhere that you were supposed to speak quietly and confidently, with no quick moves.

Suddenly the dog barked behind him—a startling, rapid warning that made goose bumps pop out on his arms. The warning slowed to deep growls, and then, to Harley's amazement, ended in an uncertain *"Wook!"* They stared at each other through the next lightning flash. *"Wook!"* the dog warned again, sounding as phony as Vernie trying to bluster her way out of a bad situation.

"Okay," Harley agreed softly. "Okay. I'm leaving. Finish your fish bones or whatever. You've had a rough day." In the next flash of lightning, he could see that the dog's white face had a black island in it, containing an eye and an ear. Below it was a neck like a linebacker's, and wide-spreading legs.

One good thing: those legs had to be tired. Harley backed away toward the road. To his horror, the dog came slowly toward him. He gripped the duffel, ready to swing, and culled his memory. You held out your hand. The dog either sniffed it and knew you were friendly, or had it for supper. He stretched out his stiff fingers. The dog eased a few steps closer, warily ducking its muzzle.

Finally Harley felt the dog's dry nose test his fingers. It took its time—smelling cheese sandwich, probably. Very slowly he let his hand ease between the white ear and the black ear, and down its back. He could feel short, slick hair on a body as hard and tight as a giant sausage.

A body that was trembling.

Harley carefully drew his hand back. "You're as scared as I am, you dumb reject." The dog respectfully sniffed his knee, then his crotch and other knee. Its white-tipped tail swung back and forth a moment, then tucked again as the thunder cracked.

Rain began to thump around them. Harley sized up the picnic table. He'd just be sitting in mud if he crawled under it and the rain poured down for long. The dog waited at a safe distance. He tried to remember if you stayed away from trees or out of empty spaces in a lightning storm.

"Maybe you've got instincts for this, but I don't," he told the dog. "All I know is I've got to have a *roof*." He flinched as the lightning turned everything momentarily pink.

But in the flash, he had seen it. Just across the road. Not only was it a roof—it was a complete little building, with a door.

He ran for it, wishing a warm, dry bed could be waiting inside, but since it was less than half the size of a bed, all he could count on was a seat with a hole in it.

He let the door slam and stood breathing hard in the dark. Rain pelted the roof as he scooted his feet along the gritty floor, hoping he wasn't sharing his refuge with scorpions or snakes or those Gila monster things that looked like Vernie's beaded costumes. Nothing seemed to move. He was going to have to lie down eventually, but he dreaded it.

He thought he heard a scratching at the door, but he said to it, "No. You're not my problem." He dried his wet face and hair with toilet paper and tried not to breathe the odor drifting up from the privy's pit below him.

Then he heard a little moan of loneliness, and his fingers suddenly fumbled to unlatch the door and let the dog come in.

For a while they jockeyed uncertainly for places to lie, but finally curled close together in two damp, cramped crescents. He could feel the dog's heat, and its trembles at each thunderclap. When it suddenly released a jet of acrid gas, like some kind of terrible air freshener, a huge laugh surged through Harley's clinched body and lowered him into sleep.

It was light when the dog woke him, wanting out. As it hurried off to lift its leg, Harley pivoted stiffly in the rain-washed road, trying to decide which way to go. The dog watched, then followed as he started off.

A Jeep came rumbling toward them. The driver had on a uniform. Harley gulped in apprehension as it came to a stop. The man said, "You need to have your dog on a leash, son."

"It's not mine," Harley said. "Some guys left it out here yesterday—they blasted off, with it trying to catch up. I'm just giving it a walk."

The man looked down at the dog's old, well-chewed collar with no tags on it and sighed. "Yeah. Lots of clowns get the idea a place like this is a good dumping ground. You want me to take him?"

The dog eased closer to Harley, panting so hard its jaws made a six-inch smile. Harley stared back into its intense eyes uneasily. The man's answer somehow made the dog's abandonment seem official. Carefully he said, "We were just getting our appetites worked up for breakfast."

The man smiled. "He's thirsty, too. Give him some water." He pointed to a faucet in another picnic area Harley had just passed. Harley went hot as he remembered the dog's long race behind the pickup. "Or at least think to give him some as soon as you get back to your campsite."

"Right," Harley said. "Daddy's got a big bowl I can use."

Oh, man, he thought as the Jeep took off. What am I doing? I couldn't even hand the stupid dog over to him!

When the man was out of sight, they went back to the tap. The dog drank until it bulged like a water balloon. "Sorry about that," Harley told it, filling his own empty stomach with water, too. "I'm dumb!" He felt miserable. Besides being hungry and stiff and lost, here he suddenly had this dog, and no idea how he was going to rustle up food and a ride.

And even if somebody should stop to pick him up, and asked where he was headed, what would he say?

They walked for maybe a mile. The dog sprinted through the brush, its pointed ears alert, checking holes in the damp soil as if each one might contain breakfast. Then Harley heard a car approaching from behind them. Something told him who it was, but he walked on without looking back.

The station wagon slowly overtook him, passed, and stopped. When he got even with the front seat, he looked in at May Woods and said, "Hi."

She rolled her eyes to heaven and then stared ahead through her streaked windshield. "I was afraid of this."

"I thought you'd be up and gone," he said.

"I should have been. But I didn't get to sleep till nearly

morning, after the rain passed." She turned to study him. "You made it, I see. Where'd you stay?"

"Don't ask," he said, hoping he didn't still smell like a night in the john.

She turned her gaze on the dog. "What is that?" The dog gave her his pink, black-rimmed smile. "Good Lord. Those jaws. He looks like an eighty-pound rattlesnake with legs."

Harley said, "I think maybe us two rejects have sort of adopted each other."

May gave him a sharp glance, then nodded. "I saw him running after that truck while I was having supper. Why would anyone be so cruel?" She hesitantly lowered her hand out the window for the dog to sniff. Its tail wagged, but it held back, wary. Suddenly she gave the steering wheel a little punch. "I can't take a dog, Harley."

He felt a surge of hope. She had practically said she could take *him*. But he said, "I wasn't asking you."

"No, really, Harley—I stopped to say I'll take you to the first town. I'll even treat you to a café breakfast, such as it may be. I feel I owe you that, somehow. I lay there all night, wondering if . . ." She looked distressed. "But no dog." She gave the steering wheel a real whack. "Look, I'm trying to help you."

He shook his head. "I know. But if we drove off and I looked back and he was running after—"

"Both of you, then!" She threw her hands apart in

surrender. "Just get in, Flotsam. And you, too, Jetsam. While I'm still out of my head."

Harley felt an elated sense of power that he had to test. "Should I ride with a crazy lady?"

"Should I take guff from a kid with toilet paper stuck to his hair?" she answered. "Get in or walk—take your choice."

He opened the back and shoved the dog between her luggage and boxes. She was right about it weighing eighty pounds. Then he got in beside May Woods. "Toilet paper?" he asked.

She picked some bits of dried tissue out of his hair and stowed them fussily in the little trash sack hanging from a knob on the dash. She said, "When I was packing up Rosabella here, to start this trip, I swore I would begin to live a new way. I would say 'Yes!' to whatever came into my life." She looked at him and the dog. "But this is ridiculous."

"*Rosabella?*" he asked in disbelief. For the first time since he'd left the coast, he let himself smile.

FOUR

They stopped and had bacon and eggs at the first truck stop they came to. She watched him eat and asked him where he had lived on the coast. He said sort of all around L.A. Then he asked her where she was from, and she said down near San Diego. She'd lived there for over thirty years. "You have a house?" he asked wistfully.

"I did. The church provided a lovely house because my husband was the music director—they adored him and couldn't do enough for him."

"Was?" he asked.

She nodded. "All that went *poof*—the house and everything."

He wasn't following her. "You two got a divorce? Or you're walking out on him, or what?"

She handed him the toast she hadn't eaten, and the tiny tub of jelly. "I'm not sure what the legal terms for it are, but *he* walked out. Flew out, actually. He has another family I didn't know about. In the Philippines or someplace in that area, where he was stationed during World War II. Before I even knew him."

"You mean like bigamy?"

Her face got stiff. "No, not two wives at the same time. Just—just another woman, and two children. That I didn't know about. For over forty years."

"Yeah?" he said, trying to imagine forty years. "When did you find out?"

"Last week. He said he had a family he wanted to go back to, and he couldn't live a lie any longer." She took a gulp of coffee. Her cup jittered when she set it down. "He cried. Then he got on a plane and disappeared. And I don't know the term for what I suddenly became."

"One real surprised sucker?" he suggested, knowing how it felt to suddenly become something new and scary.

"You have a way with words, Harley."

He shrugged. A lot of guys had bailed out on Vernie. It was one of those things.

"I feel very strange, talking about this," she said. He noticed her fingers trembled as she picked up crumbs and put them into her plate. "It's been a shock for me, a very humiliating—" She waited for her voice to even out. "I feel terribly angry and distrustful."

It was awkward, listening to her. He knew she was being nice to him and all, but he'd already used up all his emotion on his own crazy soap opera.

"Actually, you're the first person I've shared this with, Harley." She gulped the last of her coffee and made a bitter face. "I was summoned before the church board to explain. I said, 'I will not appear, because what happened is none of your snooping business!' Then I packed up Rosabella and took off."

"Good for you," he said, feeling a little tug of kinship in spite of himself. "I guess you showed them."

"Probably not. But it showed *me* that I could at least

try to take control of my life. Last evening when I realized you were doing essentially the same thing—I'm sorry, but I had to eavesdrop. I had to see if you could pull it off. It was almost as if *I* could, if you could." Unexpectedly she put her hand over his on the narrow table. "But I'm talking your ear off—when you've got as many problems as I have."

He shrugged. "And no house over the mountains to go hide in."

Her face went cool, and she got up to pay the bill. "You'll have to put the dog in an animal shelter, Harley. Then try to think of someone you can stay with for a while. Till you can decide what to do."

He gathered his courage and leaped, the way he had the day before, toward something better than that. "I've thought of a place."

They went out into the heat. "I hope it's not too far away. I have a few extra dollars to help you with a bus ticket, but if—"

"How far away is your house?"

She stopped on the sidewalk so abruptly that someone behind them nearly plowed into her. "Oh, no," she said. "Not my house. Impossible."

He tried to say it all at once. "Has somebody been living in it? Does it need cleaning and stuff? You want to pay somebody to help with all that—or get a kid free?"

She walked away from him. He followed, trying to guess what thoughts were slugging it out inside her head. He'd moved too fast.

He came up beside her. After all the years of having to ask, it still hurt. "Please, May-with-a-*y*, let us go with you."

Her stride got longer. Her face set hard.

He tried to keep his voice bright. "For a start I can keep you awake while you drive today. I owe you one for losing a night's sleep over me."

She gave him a sharp glance. "Your mother's taught you all the tricks, hasn't she? Is this how you're going to spend your life, Harley—living off your charm and other people?"

He stopped on the sunbaked sidewalk. "Jeez, why do you think I'm standing here in What's-Its-Name, Arizona, with forty dollars in my pocket and a disposable dog? I'm *trying* to do it different!"

They glared at each other, testing their strengths. He could see how troubled her eyes were in her suspicious face, and felt a twinge of pity for her. But on the other hand, *she* had a place to go.

She turned down a street and went into a supermarket. He followed anxiously as she selected a bunch of bananas. Then she picked up a yellow plastic bowl and a carton of pretend meat mashed into red patties. Dog food.

He couldn't stand the suspense any longer. As she paid for her purchases, he asked, "What's that stuff supposed to mean?"

"This stuff is supposed to mean that poor old Ishmael, waiting back there in Rosabella, can eat and drink." Before his eyes could pop, she grasped his arm firmly.

"But I am going to have to take this situation one day at a time, Harley. Maybe one mile at a time."

"Sure," he said in a burst of hopefulness. "That's fair. But that means I can keep him—right?" All at once, to his surprise, that was important.

She strode toward the street where she had parked, still looking shaken by what she'd done. But she took a deep breath and said, "All three of us might as well begin our new-and-improved lives at the same time."

"Right!" He almost danced behind her. "What was that name you said?"

"Ishmael? There was an Ishmael in the Bible who was sent out into the desert. Exiled there with his mother, actually."

"It's too long," he decided. "Maybe Ish."

"Why not?" she said. "I don't suppose he was left out at the lake because he's sick or anything like that. He looks like a nice, strong, healthy dog. Not vicious, or the kind that chews everything to shreds when he's left alone by him—"

They looked at each other and suddenly began to run.

The dog was lolling behind the steering wheel like a bored chauffeur. When it saw them it stood up, forgetting to pant. Its head went down, and its tail made a couple of apologetic sweeps.

A few scraps of the cookie sack were scattered in the back of the station wagon, along with the mangled stem of what had once been grapes. For dessert the dog had chewed on the handle of the thermos.

"You stupid idiot!" Harley yelled. What it had done was probably going to get them left stranded on a hot sidewalk like two beached jellyfish.

He peered through the windows. May's luggage seemed to be intact. The seats weren't gnawed. He waited for her to unlock the door so he could haul the dog out and give it hell. But she took her time, fishing in her purse as she surveyed the damage.

"I'll get you for this!" he promised through the glass.

She found her keys. "No, you won't. He was hungry, and you don't pass up a meal when you don't know where the next one is coming from." She sighed. "He left the spigot on the jug. See if it still works. Give him some tea. Then drain him over there in the vacant lot before we start."

Harley obeyed, dizzy with apprehension. Under his breath he told the dog what he thought of it. It stared into the distance with its head tucked down. When he reached for it, to stuff it back into Rosabella, it flinched as if it expected a whack.

May had put her glasses on and was puzzling over a map when Harley got in. He didn't know what to say about the damage to her jug and food. He couldn't believe she was letting it pass.

Her fingers traced a highway across miles of what looked like empty space. At last, she folded the map and took off her glasses. She didn't even mention the dog. "Well, Harley, you're cheaper to talk to than a psychiatrist. And it's true the house has been rented a long,

long time and will need cleaning—maybe even repairs."
Unexpectedly she smiled at him. "Do you do windows?"

"I never did. But I never did any of this." He smiled
back.

"Then we might as well give it a try. But in a week,
or whenever the house is ready, you've got to move on,
Harley. You've got to have it figured out by then. Understood?"

"Yes," he said. A week wasn't much, but it beat what
he'd had an hour ago.

May drove out of town. She started a tape, and a huge
orchestra began to blare out something for Rosabella to
waltz to. Up ahead the hot road shimmered. Harley
sighed and allowed his body to slump at last.

In spite of his promise to keep May awake, he fell
asleep against the vibrating glass of his window. He woke
to find that May had parked at a rest stop and was nap-
ping, too, propped in her corner. He stared at her, ready
to shift his gaze if she stirred. She looked worn out.

But when she did wake up, she patted her hair into
place and was off again, acting chipper and humming
along with her operatic music. She told him all about the
Anasazi and cliff dwellings and a whole little country
called the Navajo Nation up north of the highway. None
of it made much sense to him, but he kept a listening
look on his face and said, "Yeah?" a lot.

Inside his head he gently took out his memories of
Daddy and sifted them. Daddy off to paint a house, with
his ladders and scaffolding tied to the van. Daddy stirring

up supper with one hand and holding the phone with the other, while his pot holder scorched somewhere and his big, tired, rumbling laugh drowned out the world.

In his mind Harley let the two of them fall in front of the TV with their piled plates and rented movies. They disappeared into the long-ago time Daddy liked best, the King Arthur hero-and-brave-deed time that left them both teary-eyed.

I wish you could take me in again, he told the gray drift of memory.

Suddenly he realized May was telling about a place where you could stand in four states at one time. He murmured, "No kidding."

May said, "I should have gone the northern route and shown you Mesa Verde and the Grand Canyon."

"It's okay—I've probably seen it on TV." He was pretty sure he had, even if he couldn't remember what a Mesa Verde was.

"TV and movies aren't real life. You're staring at a picture—someone's interpretation—instead of participating!" she told him sternly.

"So your kids didn't get to watch, I bet," he said, put off by her snippy schoolteacher voice. Those nights at Daddy's, gobbling up spaghetti and horror and sex and car crashes, might have been interpretations, but they were as real as he could take.

She drove in silence a few seconds. "I never had children," she said finally. He waited. Was he supposed to say "Too bad," or "Good thinking," or what? "My husband felt . . . His work was his whole life, you see, and he didn't . . ." Her voice faded out.

Didn't want his life cluttered up, he thought. Two trucks slowly overtook and passed them, making Rosabella shudder.

"Were you ever sorry?" he asked, feeling Vernie's grip on his shirtfront.

It seemed like a simple question, but she slowed down, turned off the highway, and rattled across the cattle guard of a faint ranch road. "I loved him. So I wanted what he wanted," she said. "Walk the dog."

He got out and went up the road. When he looked back, May was standing in the scrubby junipers, windblown and small. He couldn't tell if she was resting from driving, or crying, or putting the whammy on old Nolan, or what, but it gave him and the dog an opportunity to go behind a bush.

When he threw a small stick out tentatively for it to fetch, it brought back a tree branch instead, crunching off bark and splinters in its excitement. "You're a dummy, Ish," he said, testing the sound of the name. The dog whipped the branch back and forth as easily as a twig, and rapped Harley hard across the shin.

When they got back to the car, May was okay. She gave them tea, even though all the ice had melted, and they started climbing toward the pale mountains that had broken the skyline in the east.

Later she slowed down in the pine trees, where leftover snow was melting, and rolled down her window. She breathed the cold air, then asked him, "What do you want out of life, Harley?"

It was a dumber question than his had been. He shrugged and stared out his own window.

She picked up speed again. "You wanted something yesterday. Desperately."

He drew into himself like a turtle for protection. It was none of her business what he desperately wanted.

Just when he thought she had forgotten what she had been talking about, she said, "I imagine it amazed you, didn't it? That you had never questioned the way you lived, or the kind of mother you had, or where it all was heading."

He didn't answer.

She said, "And then yesterday you did question. The pain was so bad that you . . ." She tried to choose a word.

Broke, he supplied for her in his mind. Broke, like a dam that couldn't hold all the backed-up heaviness anymore.

The dog stood up behind them, panting and dripping, and stared ahead as if it were about to give directions. With his thumb Harley blotted the drops that fell on Rosabella's clean old upholstery.

What am I doing here, with a dumped dog and a nosy old lady? he asked himself. I don't need this—I'm like some stray myself, all wagging and careful so somebody'll like me and take me home.

The dog leaned over the back of the seat and licked his ear.

"Don't!" he said.

FIVE

In the night Harley woke to hear rain tapping the roof of the station wagon. At the campground May had ordered the dog up front to sleep with the luggage and boxes they had piled there to clear the back. But while they slept, bundled in all the clothes they had, against the chill, it had crept between them, and lay with its chin on May's arm. Harley reached out and touched the dog's warm, solid body. When he heard the thump of a tail in answer, he smiled and slept again.

May seemed nervous the next morning as they repacked the back and ran the dog in the fresh, cold dampness. They ate bananas and the last sandwich, drank from the campground spigot, and were on their way.

"I know it can't be the same as I remember it," she explained for about the tenth time. It was her house she was worried about. When her folks had died, she couldn't bear to sell it, so it had been a rental ever since. "Of course I realize I'm not escaping back to my childhood, where I was safe and loved. It will very likely need repairs, too. But if they're extensive, I simply won't have the money." In another voice she said, "He left me half our savings. Everything else he took. If I live very carefully, that might last me two years. Then I'll be seventy-one and broke."

He didn't know how to respond. It beat forty dollars. "Maybe his other family had it hard a long time—without him there, and all. So he wanted to make it up—"

"With money that was half mine? How generous and kind of him."

He shut up and let her be as miserable as she wanted.

She was a nervous wreck by the time they crossed the final pass and started down the eastern slope. He stared out, silent, at the peaks and streams and clouds and patches of real snow. He hadn't expected mountains to be such big suckers.

When they stopped at a drive-in for hamburgers at noon, she backed into a post. It only dented a little spot by one taillight, but she had a cow.

"Calm down," he told her.

"I know. I know. But I'm expecting too much."

"Well, why don't you just be glad you've got something to *expect*!" he said. She looked as startled as he felt, and drove on for a long time in silence.

Finally she pointed out the pale, level horizon of the plains through a gap in the foothills they were coming out of. They passed little towns perched along creeks. She tried to remember their names, getting mixed up among the new interchanges and housing developments.

All at once she said, "You've been a good companion, Harley. Thank you."

He felt awkward. Maybe she automatically said nice things, being around churches and stuff like that so long.

They went through a little town three or four blocks long. "This is called Gattman," she said. "The closest real town is Freeling, down the highway."

She turned off on a smaller, gravel road. It passed planted fields and a bunch of junky mobile homes, then rose over a hill and sank toward a creek in the distance.

A couple of miles beyond the hilltop, she suddenly turned in at a dilapidated red-brick house. Behind it was a big old garage or shed of some kind and a beat-up truck.

"Good Lord," she said.

He gathered it had changed for the worse.

"Oh, what a pity," she said. "Most of the cottonwoods are gone. I loved those trees." She got stiffly out of Rosabella and looked around at everything but the house, as if she had to brace herself. It wasn't that bad, Harley decided. The yard had been raked recently. Little piles of trash were heaped around. It was going to beat an out-house or the back of a station wagon for sleeping in.

He got out, too. Just then a loose-skinned old yellow dog came around the corner of the house and padded amiably out to them, sweeping its feathered tail. It smelled Harley's hand and ambled over to Rosabella to greet Ish, who was going crazy trying to get through a three-inch crack in the window.

"Hush!" Harley ordered over Ish's clamor. He glanced anxiously at May, then turned back to Ish. "Shut up, you idiot!"

May's face was puzzled. "There shouldn't be a dog here. I'm sure my husband would have said absolutely no pets." She shushed at it uncertainly. "Go home. Get away from there—don't you dare jump up and scratch my paint!"

A voice from somewhere called, "His name is Coo. He doesn't jump up on things."

They spun around, hunting the owner of the voice. Nothing moved but the dogs. Harley peered through the cedars that guarded the front porch, feeling spied upon. Then he realized that the yellow dog had tilted its muzzle up. He backed away from the house and looked up, too.

A tall girl stood straddling the ridge of the roof like a mountain climber, blocking the sun. She waved and began to walk down the shadowy slope toward the eaves. First her bare feet, then her jeans and baggy shirt, and finally her stringy black hair and brown face lost their outline of light. She squatted closer to the edge than Harley would have dared, and said, "Hi," with an enthusiastic smile. She pointed to the ground. "Would you pitch me my hammer? It slid off a while ago."

He found it in a clump of grass. "Just—throw it up there?"

"Sure," she said. She stood up and caught it with one hand, filling him with mixed respect and envy. May was beside him by that time, staring up. The girl said, "You must be the landlady."

"Yes. I'm May Woods. And you are?"

"Singer," the girl said. She just smiled as May waited, expecting a last name, too, the way old people did.

"You don't live here," May said, firmly enough to make it true.

The girl sat down on the warped shingles, putting the hammer behind her so it wouldn't slide. "No, ma'am. I just came to help Bill. *He* lives here."

Harley glanced at May. She had jutted her already-lifted chin. "Not anymore. I've come to move in. The realtor surely informed—who did you say?"

"Bill Bascomb," the girl said. She lifted her brown hands in a dramatic shrug. "Well, he's still here. I mean all his stuff is, not him. He's in the hospital."

May stepped backward. "He's *what?*"

"In the hospital. He fell and did something to his hip or back or something. I came over as soon as I knew about it. I figured he needed some help."

Harley moved his lips silently, matching May's *Good Lord.*

"You want to see him?" the girl asked.

"*See* him?" Now that she had the Lord's attention, May found her strength. "No, thank you very much—he's not pulling that on me. He's supposed to be out of my house. Every stick of furniture. Gone. Removed!"

The girl smiled gently. "Well, it's not." She looked down at Harley. "Why don't you let your dog out? It's hot in there. Old Coo's friendly."

Harley hesitated. "I don't know how it acts with other dogs."

"It?" the girl asked. "I wouldn't know how to act, either, if I thought I was an *it.*"

Harley flushed. "Him," he said, and mentally let her and her hammer slide off the roof together.

May fumbled in her purse and jerked out an address on a card. "I'm going to the realtor." She strode to the station wagon. "I don't have time for this man's tricks." She opened the door and was nearly flattened by Ish on his way out to demolish the other dog. She hurled his water bowl out after him, yelling, "Give him a drink!" and drove away.

Ish sprinted up and gave Coo a shove with his thick shoulder that nearly knocked the old guy off his feet. Then, with a growl and a snarling lunge, he bit Coo's lip. Coo wheeled out of reach and stopped at a distance, so perplexed that he forgot to give his tail orders to stop wagging. Ish stalked toward him again, his slitted eyes intent.

Harley froze. This could be bad. Big bad. He made his voice work. "Ish! Get back here!" Was he supposed to rush in there and pull two fighting dogs apart? "Ish!" he shouted, but the crazy bully had gone deaf.

Suddenly he felt the girl beside him. She went right past him to Ish and took his collar without hesitation. "No," she said in a low, decisive voice. "We don't fight here." She held him tight as he lunged again.

Unexpectedly Ish turned, wagging all over to make himself cute and forgiven, and licked her arm. She smiled and stroked his quivering hide. "Good boy!" she praised. She held out her free hand. "Come on back, Coo. This stranger just had a macho attack. He's sorry." She gave Ish's collar a jerk that startled him into sitting down.

Coo came to her warily. There was a little dot of blood on his lip. Even *he's* braver than I am, Harley thought.

"Aren't you ashamed?" the girl asked Ish. He lifted his nose to her, looking as pained and contrite as he could manage. "Coo wouldn't hurt a fly. You don't have to prove a thing with him." She let go of Ish's collar. The two dogs toured gingerly around each other. Then, as if he had more important things to do, Ish pranced off to explore the yard.

"I just got him," Harley said, suddenly defensive because he should have done what she just did. "How'd you know he'd mind you?"

"By looking at his face," she said, seeming surprised that he had to ask. "His expression. You can tell—just like with people. They weren't going to fight."

She filled the plastic bowl at a faucet by the front steps and smiled at Harley, who hadn't moved. It was a sweet, playful smile that he had seen before but couldn't place.

"How'd you get down so fast?" he asked uneasily.

She looked at the roof and pursed her lips. "How about if I jumped?"

He shrugged. "Okay by me." Couldn't she just *say?*

"Is that lady your grandmother?" she asked.

He could play her game. "How about if she isn't?"

The girl laughed. "What were you calling your dog?"

47

"Ish," he said. "Its name—his name—is Ishmael."

She practically beamed. "Ishmael? That's wonderful! 'God hears.' "

He backed away a few steps in case she got any weirder.

"That's what *Ishmael* means."

"Oh." He relaxed a little. "I thought it was something about getting left out in the desert."

"Oh—yeah, *that* Ishmael. He and Hagar—she was his mother—they got banished. I liked the part where here's her kid, dying of thirst out there, and Hagar suddenly sees this *well* she hasn't seen before. Do you suppose it had just that second appeared? A magic well?"

He hesitated. "All that's in the Bible?"

She laughed again. "All that's just a page or two of the, like, first chapter. Genesis."

They watched as Ish left his wet graffiti on the fence. When old Coo went back to the shade next to the house, Ish stopped exploring and found his own cool place.

"You live around here?" Harley asked.

She thought about it. "Off and on. Wherever somebody needs me. My dad's in the VA hospital, and my mom's been dead a couple of years. So I'm sort of helping out people around Gattman right now. I stayed with an old woman nearly a year, till her children put her in a nursing home. Bill calls me the local angel. I figured as long as he needs me, I'll probably stay here and make myself useful."

Suddenly he noticed a little beat-up suitcase sitting

beside the door. Something about it sent a jolt of loneliness through him. Well, join the club, he thought.

"I saw a rake, so I've been cleaning up a little. Then I found some shingles blown off. So I went up to try to knock them back in. We've got some patching to do. But we'll need some roofing cement."

"We?" he said. We don't waste much time, do we?

She smiled up at the roof. "Don't you get a bang out of being up high?" She lifted her arms as she slowly revolved, flapping them like some kind of loony bird fixing to take off. "Feeling all that love out there, coming at you like radiation or something, is wonderful."

He backed off a little farther. She definitely was weird. Down on the ground she seemed plainer than when she had stood outlined against the sun. Her face was grubby, and she didn't have a bit of makeup on, even though he figured she was sixteen or so. He wasn't sure he could get friendly with anybody who caught hammers one-handed and waded in to stop dogfights, but maybe so. She had an easy way of talking, as if she had known him for a long time.

Still, he envied the way Ish had arrived, settled who was top dog, and stretched out to rest.

The girl said, "How about raking some, while we wait?"

Oh, man. It was starting already. He knew working was what he was there for—he'd made a bargain. But May ought to be the one telling him. "How about me waiting, while you do it?" he asked, stalling.

She laughed. "I know. It's hard to get passionate about dog doo and dandelions." She filled a cardboard box with debris and carried it off. The dogs got up and followed her, leaving him standing awkwardly alone.

She came back and raked some more while Harley watched. Finally in irritation he said, "This guy's not really sick, is he?"

"Bill? He fell and pulled something. Ligaments or something. I don't think he broke any bones. Maybe a fracture. I didn't see him—I just talked to his nurse."

"How long's he going to be in there? He can't leave all his stuff here in May's house."

"The nurse said he can probably come home in three or four days." She considered what she had said. "Well, not come *home*, I guess."

"Didn't he know he had to get out?"

She made a don't-ask-me face. "All I know is, old Coo wasn't being fed, and things needed looking after. So I came."

She filled her box again. He glanced down the road where May had disappeared. "She's moving in," he said, determined to get through to the girl. "She's been driving three days, from the West Coast, and she's not about to wait for some guy to get his ligaments back together. She'll set his stuff out in the yard."

The girl laughed and lifted her eyebrows. "She doesn't know Bill."

Before he could ask what needed to be known, he saw Rosabella coming in a jet stream of dust.

"Where's her own furniture?" the girl asked.

He tried to think. "Maybe it's coming. Or maybe it belonged with her old house, and she'll have to get new stuff." That didn't seem right—May hadn't sounded like she had that kind of money anymore. "Maybe from garage sales, or something," he finished, going tense as Rosabella roared toward them.

The girl nodded. "Well, brace yourself," she said cheerfully. "I think the fireworks are about to start."

SIX

"Unbelievable!" May exclaimed, striding stern-faced up the steps to the porch. Harley and the girl and both dogs gathered behind her. "The realtor didn't even have a key! Am I supposed to break my own window and crawl in?"

The girl eased past her and opened the screen door. When she turned the tarnished doorknob, the heavy wooden door swung back into the house with a faint meow. "Bill's not much of a door locker," she explained.

Coo went in first like a good host, then turned to welcome them with dignified sweeps of his tail. May took an audible breath and stepped inside. Harley heard a louder gasp. Then she said, "I don't *believe* this," in a hollow voice. He squeezed inside and looked around.

Bill wasn't much of a housekeeper, either.

The room looked like a compacted thrift store. It wasn't very large, for a living room, but three couches and four big chairs were stuffed into it. Their seats were piled with boxes, tools, window shades, shoes, empty picture frames, and plain old trash. What looked like a dining room table was buried under more boxes and car parts and apple juice jugs and little towers of junk mail. Smaller pieces of furniture filled the rest of the room, leaving a little trail to wind through. Under it all were rugs laid on top of other rugs.

"This can't be real," May whispered. She looked like she needed to sit down, but there wasn't an empty spot. She edged across the room, starting an avalanche of letters and aluminum cans from the table. The clatter sent Ish skittering out from under it with cobwebs draped between his sharp, scared ears.

The girl picked up some of the cans, then seemed to see the hopelessness of what she was doing. She grinned at Harley and flipped them over her shoulders without even looking back to see where they landed. The unexpectedness of it almost startled a laugh out of him. But another exclamation of pain from May sobered him up. She had discovered the kitchen.

He wound through the clutter and leaned in at the kitchen door. May was standing in the middle of another riot area. Besides the usual stove, refrigerator, cabinets, and counters, the room was crammed with an overflowing bookcase and a desk loaded with the fenders and radiator from some really old car.

"Bill's a collector," the girl whispered behind him.

"Of what?" he asked. "One of everything there is?"

She giggled. May opened the refrigerator and glared at the containers full of gray sludge and unrecognizable lumps. "People can't live like this," she said in a dazed voice.

"Well, he had to leave unexpectedly, you know," the girl gently reminded her. "And he's been gone—I don't know how many days. It won't take us long to clean it up."

Harley opened a cabinet door. A pile of old fast-food cartons fell out and plopped into a big pan of dingy water on the counter. He gingerly rescued the driest ones, and held up the dripping ones, hunting a trash can or waste-basket.

May looked around, too. "There isn't any. He's never thrown anything away."

The girl laughed. It was a free, natural cackle with a little squeak at the end that Harley liked in spite of himself. Since the whole house seemed to be one big trash can, he let the cartons drop back into the water.

"This is shocking to me," May said to the girl. "My mother kept this house spotless when I lived here. I can't—this—look what he's *done* to it."

The girl gazed around sympathetically. "You must really have nice memories of how it was. I guess Bill lives in a different way." She found a pile of plastic bags and dropped some rotten apples and potato peels into one of them. "This can be for compost." She opened another one. "I expect he's saving all this plastic and cans and stuff to recycle. When he goes to some town that'll take it." She began to clear the countertops briskly, scraping old jar lids and greasy hamburger wrappers into a third sack.

The stunned look slowly faded from May's face as she watched. She asked in a different voice, "What did you say your name was?"

"Not *was*," the girl said pleasantly. "Is. It's Singer." She narrowly missed stepping into a skillet on the floor beside Coo's water pan. It had been licked so clean that she picked it up and said, "Hey, we won't have to wash this one." May blanched. "Kidding." The girl laughed, and added it to the dirty dishes piled in the sink.

"He's going to hire someone to clean this house," May declared. "Or it's coming out of his deposit." She stopped, holding a cantaloupe rind. "If there was a deposit."

"I don't know if Bill has that kind of money," Singer said softly. "But I don't mind doing it." She looked into a stuffed cabinet. "Bill shouldn't object if we make some supper from whatever we can find, since he's putting you out so much. Here's some chili. But it's kind of dented. I guess it's marked down when it's dented. Here's some pineapple chunks."

May touched Harley's shoulder. "I think we should see what the chances are of spending the night in real beds." She started out, but he was too dense to follow until she added, "Harley, will you help me, please?"

He and Ish followed her into a bedroom crowded with cedar chests and dressers and old trunks heaped with blankets and dirty clothes. She beckoned him close.

"Who *is* this little strange creature?" she whispered. "Is she *staying* here? Am I supposed to feed her? I thought we would go get something at a drive-in in Gattman, but *three* of us—"

"She's staying," Harley said. A red kite—tail and all—tacked to the ceiling above the bed, grabbed his attention. "She works for people around here, and came to help Bill."

May sighed and gazed around. Piles of books and magazines and potato chips were already at rest on the unmade bed. Dog hairs had gathered in drifts around the legs and bottoms of the furniture, and Coo had left a small gnawed bone on the rug. Ish immediately helped himself to it. "No!" May exclaimed. "Get him out!"

Singer magically appeared and led Ish and his prize away.

May closed her eyes. "I'm tired," she said in a shaky voice. "All I can think of is food and a hot bath and a bed."

Harley went into the next room. All it contained was a big bed, some boxes stacked along one wall, and a tall floor lamp wearing a cowboy hat.

"I think he forgot he had this one, May," he called. "It's better."

She came in. "Well, thank goodness." Her face softened. "This was my room." She turned back the flowered spread to check the sheets. "Amazing." She went to the window and pushed back the curtains, which were only a little gray. She stared out—hunting for how it had been, he guessed.

He hoped there were more sleeping places still lurking in the junk somewhere, even though he'd sleep with the potato chips if he had to—anything would beat the back of Rosabella.

"Is the old guy really hurt?" he asked.

"The realtor said he fell, a few days ago. Tripped over a skillet, probably." She went into a little hall. "I would have had an accident, too, just to get out of this—this squalor."

She peeped into the bathroom, and backed away with her mouth pinched up. He looked in, too, to check out what squalor might be there, but it just looked like an ordinary bathroom. Except, come to think about it, most ordinary ones didn't have a smiling moose head, life-size but made out of fake fur, mounted on the wall with towels and washcloths hanging from its antlers.

May started toward the kitchen, then seemed to realize she hadn't settled what to do with Singer in there, sloshing away at the dirty dishes. She turned back to Harley uncertainly. He shrugged, and said, "Let's just have the dented chili."

May pressed her weary eyes. "I suppose that's the simplest. I will not bring fresh food into this house until that kitchen is clean." She went in. Singer was drying a pile of plates while the pots and pans soaked in her sinkful of suds. Something smelled good.

"I started the chili. The top of the can wasn't bulged out, but I'll boil it good anyway, so it'll be safe."

"It's a wonder he didn't kill himself three times a day," May said.

"I found some carrots that are a little limber to eat raw. So I'm cooking them, too. There's crackers. We'll feel a lot better when we eat." Singer smiled as May attacked the table with a battered sponge and cleaning powder. "Did you find sleeping places?"

"One not so good," Harley said. "One better."

"That's great." She beamed as if he had invented box springs. "I hope there're some clean sheets. I think I'll just fold one and use it on a couch in the living room. There's a little daybed on the back porch. You and Ish would probably like the porch. If you move the junk that's on the bed, I'll make it up fresh."

Curious, he went out to the breezy screened-in room off the kitchen and began to shove stuff under the bed. Compared to his last two sleeping places, it was luxurious.

May came out, too, and stared through the screen at the yard. "Yes. That's the old cottonwood. Only there used to be five more, by the shed. What a pity they've gone." She noticed what she was leaning against. "Oh, look, there's a washing machine under here. I wonder if it works."

"It will," Singer called from the kitchen. "We'll *make* it work."

May murmured, "Is she hoping to be voted Miss Positive Thinking?"

"I heard that." Singer laughed. "Come and eat."

They went in. She had set the scrubbed table with clean mismatched dishes. She pitched Ish a scrap of carrot. He gulped it, then smiled worshipfully at her. They were going to be a pair, Harley thought. Miss Too-Good-to-Be-True and God Hears.

Singer tossed another bit of carrot to Coo, but he apologetically spit it out, so she threw him a cracker. He snapped, missing it completely, and hadn't found it between his big feet before Ish shouldered him aside and gobbled it up.

"We've got a learning experience ahead, haven't we, Coo?" she said, rubbing his droopy ears. They found seats on two boxes and a wooden keg. Singer gestured at their supper. "Well, thanks, Bill."

As if it didn't matter in the least, May asked, "How long have you known this Mr. Bascomb, ah—"

"Singer," Harley supplied.

Singer laughed. "Oh, forever." A little flick of her fork sent a carrot disk flying into May's plate. "Whoops, sorry." She leaned over, stabbed it, and popped it in her mouth. "But I really got to know him last fall when I stayed down the road with the Maloneys. They had a new baby, and Juana was sick, so I stayed with them awhile to help out. I'd go into town with Bill sometimes to get their groceries and things. Or he'd take Juana in to the doctor. Because Al—Mr. Maloney—he's a trucker and was gone a lot."

May dropped a cracker into her chili and delicately held it under. "You're not having chili?" she asked suspiciously, noticing Singer's plate of carrots. Harley stopped eating. Did she know something they didn't?

"Oh, it's good. I tested it. It's just—I don't eat meat. I guess I'm too tenderhearted. I like being alive so much, I guess I figure everything else does, too."

"Ah-ha. But you're not too tenderhearted to kill carrots?" May asked, poking down the pale corpse of her cracker that had bobbed up again.

"Well, actually I am. I've really had to struggle with it," Singer said brightly. "Finally I figured, hey, the reason we eat each other is so we'll see we're all so mixed together that we're really one thing. All of us. Everything. Like, I eat carrots, so they become part of me, in my bones or whatever, and when I decay and carrots grow where I was, I'm part of them."

Harley choked and spewed a few crumbs, wondering who had decayed to produce the carrots he had just swallowed.

May's eyebrows rose. "I prefer to think we humans become much more than compost at our death."

"Oh, we're *already* much more," Singer explained. "We're wonderful and amazing. And so is compost."

Harley said, "Nothing eats people."

"Worms," Singer said. "Sharks, bacteria, maggots, mold—"

"Please!" May said. "Didn't we eliminate all that with good tight caskets?"

"Exactly." Singer nodded. "We said, 'If we can't take it with us, we'll at least lock it up.' That's really selfish and irresponsible, isn't it, not to give back even our minerals."

Harley caught himself staring at her. She couldn't be argued with. She just kept agreeing until she won.

But May wasn't finished. "You may regret not eating something more substantial. Tomorrow is going to be a backbreaker."

"How come?" Harley asked uneasily.

"Because my house is not a landfill, and I want it clean. And since a merciful providence has seen fit to supply two sets of ready hands, we're going to carry out everything we can lift and put it in the shed back there. Then we'll scrub this room. No one's feet should stick to a kitchen floor."

Under the table Harley lifted his shoes one at a time and felt the faint Velcro grip of greasy muck.

"Then the bathroom, then all the rest—walls, ceilings, floors, windows, closets—until we've eradicated every trace of Mr. Bascomb."

Harley and Singer glanced at each other. She said, "Looks like Bill is in for a shock."

"I'm the one who is shocked," May replied. "A procrastinating little man has tried to pull the ground out from under me. I'm sorry, but he's not going to do it. I have a life to get on with, and I'm getting on with it in this house, starting tonight. If you want to back out—either of you—this is the time."

Harley gave her a who-me? shrug, startled by her new-and-improved boldness. Singer smiled and said, "You better get the first bath, May. You did all that driving, and you're the tiredest." Her smile got bigger. "And the angriest. Being mad can really take the fizz out of you, can't it?"

"You know," May said sharply, "you are a disconcerting little person."

"I know," Singer agreed. "Don't feel rushed about figuring me out. It takes some people ages." She got up, expertly stepping around the dogs, who sprang up beside her, eyeing the dirty dishes in her hands. "Nope," she told them. "From now on you have your own bowls and that's it. This place is under new management."

May bristled but cleared the rest of the table, down to the last chili spatter. She said, "Harley, if you'll get the tan suitcase, please. And your duffel. We'll bring in the rest tomorrow, when the place is clean." She looked around tiredly. "Or *whenever* it's clean."

He went out through the back porch. Ish cautiously followed Coo through the little swinging door cut in the wall, and halfheartedly explored the fenced-in backyard, making sure Harley didn't get into Rosabella and drive off without him. The sun had set behind the mountains, turning each peak a different shade of hazy blue. The air was cool and—he tried to think of a word—empty. Of everything. Sounds. Smog. Ocean mist. Growing up in this bright air must have helped make May the queen of clean.

She was gone when he went back in. Water was running in the bathroom. Singer said, "I knew she'd scrub the tub and basin and toilet before she got her bath, even if she was last, so I figured why not let her do it for everybody. If you'll wash our supper dishes, I'll make up your bed."

Harley said, "I thought I'd run the dogs," to test her.

"You're not much for chores, are you?" she asked, pushing a bottle of detergent into his hand.

"Never had to be." He liked it better when she was upsetting May and leaving him alone.

She studied his face awhile. "Let's don't act with each

other. It wastes time. And while we're here, we ought to pitch in."

He hesitated, then nodded, surprised to feel relieved.

She started hot water in the sink. "Wash, rinse, drain. Have fun. I'm hunting sheets."

When she was out of sight, he dumped the things they had used into the water without detergent, fished them out, and perched them in Bill's rusty drainer. Out *you'll* go, tomorrow, he warned it. And then—he remembered with a thud of anxiety—when this place was shiny and he was the last piece of junk, out *he'd* go, too.

Singer passed through on her way to the porch. "I found clean blankets. Out here you'll need a couple if you don't want your knees to knock. You've come up in the world, Harley. To five thousand feet."

He followed her out. He might as well observe bed making, along with the geography lesson.

She flopped a folded sheet open and let it settle like a parachute on the bed. "How do you fit into all this?" she asked. "You don't act like you've known May very long."

"I don't fit into anything," he said. "And I've known May just about forty-eight hours." It felt longer. He was amazed at how much they had said to each other. More than he and Vernie talked in a month.

"So you two met as she was coming here, right? Were you hitchhiking?"

"Sort of." Being straightforward with her was harder than he expected. "I needed a ride, and she needed somebody to help her get settled here, so we made a deal."

She whacked a pillow and held it with her chin while she drew a pillowcase up around it. He felt her eyes on him in the dimness. "Well. I thought if you don't have a special destination, I'd try to help find lots of things to do, to keep you here. Okay? We might stretch it out a month, from the looks of this place."

"Jeez—yeah. Show me how to stay as long as I can." A rush of loneliness caught him unguarded. It was something evenings did to him sometimes—what they called homesickness, maybe. He felt Ish bounce up on the bed behind him, and turned in a little panic to catch at his thick shoulders, pretending to scuffle with him.

Singer said, "Why don't you get the next bath?" She gave Ish a friendly scoot so she could turn the top of the sheet down. "May's sort of a fun old lady, isn't she? Just a little hard to take at the moment." She began to giggle. "I want her to have a really good night's sleep before she finds out the shed she's planning to put everything in is already stuffed to the roof with more of Bill's junk."

SEVEN

Harley woke with his face mashed against the wall. It took him a minute to remember where he was. Then he realized Ish was stretched out in the middle of the bed, comfortably gnawing a breakfast bone from somewhere.

"Hey," he protested, too surprised to think, and shoved Ish off onto the floor. Ish immediately leaped back on the bed and stood on him, his whole body wagging in greeting. His nose poked into Harley's hair and ears, carrying the smell of barbecue sauce.

Harley jolted in a silent laugh. He'd never gotten a big production number before, just for waking up. He wasn't sure how to respond, but gave Ish some awkward little shoves and jabs.

Ish nuzzled him back and settled on his pillow. "I've got me a dog," he whispered. It hadn't sunk in until that moment. Then he thought, And we don't have anyplace to live. He lay motionless, gazing into space, as warm breath tickled his ear.

Far off he heard a chicken. Rooster. Whatever. It really did say cock-a-doodle-doo.

Then inside the house he heard May suddenly yell out the expression *she* was becoming famous for: "Good Lord!" A second later she exclaimed, "Harley—help me."

He was already hopping into the kitchen before he got

his feet into the legs of his jeans. They nearly collided. May was clutching a robe she hadn't put on, and pointing back toward something that had shocked the color out of her face.

"What!" he gasped.

"This can't be real," she said hoarsely, grabbing his arm. "I started through the other bedroom to get an early start. And he's in there."

"Who?" He was completely confused. "Coo?"

"Yes—Coo, too!" She shook him angrily. "With him!"

"With *who?*" Then it dawned on him. "Bill?" His voice dropped in amazement. "The old guy's *here?* Are you sure?"

"Who else would that lumbering dog be curled up next to?" She pushed him toward the bedroom door. "Get in there. Find out if he's drugged, or asleep, or dead or what."

"*You* find out." He grabbed for the handle of the refrigerator as he was trundled past it.

"I can't go in there. He's in his underwear. And I'm in my—" She turned him loose and yanked her robe on over her droopy pink pajamas. "Go!" she ordered.

Harley eased into the dim room. On the far side of the bed, Coo lifted his head and let it drop again. On the near side, a long knobby-kneed body was stretched out as if it had been knocked cold. Both big toes stuck out of holes in black socks. Harley took a few steps closer. He could make out a dark tattoo twining around a belly button above the waistband of polka-dotted shorts. A chest with a little pad of gray hair on it was slowly going up and down.

"Bill?" Harley whispered. "Mr. Bascomb?"

A long tanned face topped with rumpled hair turned toward him.

"Are you okay?" Harley asked.

Bill nodded without opening his eyes. He was younger than Harley had been imagining. A few years younger than May, anyway. He sighed and said in a cranky voice, "What is this—a bus station? Get out of here." His watery blue eyes finally opened and fixed on Harley.

Harley stumbled backward a couple of steps, first over Ish, then over the clothes and shoes Bill had dropped beside the bed. He jerked his hand toward the kitchen. "She wasn't expecting you—you scared her. They said you had to stay in the hospital three or four days. How'd you get here?"

Bill tried to look toward the kitchen without lifting his head. Harley caught a glimpse of May's robe disappearing as she backed out of sight. Bill said tiredly, "I take it I'm now in the clutches of the landlady from sunny Cal." He sighed. "Tell her I tippy-toed out of the hospital over in Freeling in the wee hours this morning while both nurses were putting out the little fire I started in my bedpan. You can take sick and die in those places if you're not careful. So I caught a ride as far as the Maloneys' with the man who delivers papers."

"Yeah?" he asked, impressed. "But how'd you get in here without the dogs barking or anything?"

Bill sighed again. "Juana Maloney gave me a sack of bones she'd saved for Coo. Al Maloney brought me home on his way to Kansas City. I gave bones to Coo and some three-headed guardian of Hades he had with him. Somebody was sleeping on my back porch. So I came in here and went to bed, too. And I plan to sleep ten hours straight. So shut the door on your way out." Bill closed his eyes.

Harley took another step back. "Aren't you cold?"

Bill's eyes didn't open. "Yes. I'm cold."

Harley moved a pile of magazines and some books, and pulled two blankets out from under Coo. He spread them over Bill.

Bill's hand eased out stiffly and rested on Coo's broad head. "Thank you," he said, sounding surprised.

Harley went back into the kitchen. Singer was standing behind May, dressed in yesterday's grubby clothes and glowing.

"He's back!" she whispered. "How's he feeling?"

"Good enough to get here, I guess," Harley said. He turned to May. "He just decided to walk out—"

"I heard." She sounded calmer. But her jaw jutted. "How could he have the *nerve* to come in here and make himself at home? I ought to call the hospital—or the police. Somebody."

"Might be tricky, with no phone," Singer reminded her.

May threw up her hands. She was so mad, she found a can of coffee and dumped some into a coffeepot she hadn't even scrubbed. She yanked her robe tighter and straightened her back. "Well—this isn't changing the plans for today. Everything in this room goes into the shed so we can get to work. Also Mr. Bascomb will then have everything in one spot for packing and moving."

Harley looked at Singer. She said, "You tell her."

"What?" May asked. She found an unopened jar of jelly and spread some on a cracker left from supper.

"The shed's full," Harley said. "Stuffed to the roof."

May's cracker snapped. "You're not serious." She stared at both of them. "You are. All right. Everything into the backyard."

Singer glanced at the closed bedroom door. "Even things that might ruin if it rains or hails?"

May closed her eyes wearily. "Very well. Food on the back porch—anything not waterproof. The rest outside: the desk, bookcase, car carcass—" She turned toward the door, and her voice got more distinct. "And when Mr. Bascomb has rested sufficiently, we will discuss removing *all* his belongings from the premises without any further delay. Now, we have things to do."

She was right. They did. She pinned a towel around a broom and began to wipe the ceiling. Harley's heart sank. It was going to be a top-to-bottom attack.

They emptied the cabinets and refrigerator, moved out the furniture, and took down the dingy curtains. Singer worked quickly, nodding as May gave orders. Harley did what he was told, growing more awkward and resentful each time they showed him how to scrub or scour or sort better than he was doing it. About three hours into the battle, Coo barked to be let out of the closed-up bedroom. He and Ish gazed up hopefully at Harley as he washed a window. "What!" he asked, annoyed.

"Oh, we forgot to feed them!" Singer cried. She found Coo's sack of dry food on the back porch. She couldn't find a bowl, but in seconds they were ravenously scooting food around on a newspaper. It bothered Harley that he hadn't remembered. This new responsibility stuff hadn't been in the picture when he walked off into his new life that night at the lake.

Singer peeped in at Bill. "Are you awake?" she asked softly. "Hi, it's me. Do you need anything? Are you hungry?" She must have had a head shake for an answer, because she said, "Okay. But yell if you need me." She closed the door and went back to work.

May sniffed in irritation. She grabbed a little packet of hard black lumps Harley was holding and read the label. "Dried apricots? They've got to be twenty years old! Pathetic."

At noon they had just begun to fight. But they needed reinforcements. May went to the nearest drive-in and brought back hamburgers and drinks.

"I persuaded them to make a cheeseburger without meat," she told Singer as she brought lunch out of a big sack. "I don't think anything died in its production." She drew out a fourth hamburger and drink. "Do you suppose Mr. Bascomb could be lured out of his coma a few minutes to eat this?"

Singer beamed. "May, all this is really kind of you. I bet he could be. I'll ask." She took it into the bedroom, then came out smiling. "He says to thank you, May."

"I would like to speak to him," May said.

"I know. But he's still pretty woozy. He's going to eat and then sleep some more." She looked around brightly. "But we're getting this room stirred up good while we're waiting, aren't we?" Between bites of cheeseburger, she dumped the contents of a drawer into a box. Twine, tools, clothespins, knives, seeds, pretty rocks, and rawhide bones tumbled in together.

"I hope 'clean' and 'organized' describe it better," May said. " 'Stirred up' makes it sound as though it will take a week."

Singer glanced at Harley. "Maybe even longer. The way that faucet's leaking, we may need a new one. And the curtain rod was just screwed into the wallboard. It'll pull out again unless we fix it right."

Harley's hand stopped on the wall he was washing. Was she going to ask if he could fix it? He might not make it through a full *day* here, much less the month she'd promised.

But May turned to Singer. "Can you put in faucets?"

"Sure. I love repairing things. Don't you?"

"My father mostly taught me about gardening," May said.

Singer smiled. "My mother taught me. Because my father had other things. And I read up on whatever she didn't know."

My father had other things, too, I guess, Harley thought. And you wouldn't want to know what my mother taught me.

May suddenly cringed away from the sink. A big gray spider had fallen into it and was trying to crawl up the slick side. With a gasp she lunged forward again, opened the faucet full strength, and sent the spider, drenched and flattened, down the drain.

"Oh, don't do that!" Singer exclaimed. "Please don't!" She scrunched over the sink, holding the last mashed bite of her cheeseburger in rigid fingers. "It wasn't bothering anything—we disturbed where it lived."

May stared at her in amazement. "It disturbed *me* where *I* live," she said pointedly. "I don't like spiders and won't have them in my house."

Singer bit her lip and batted pain from her eyes. She said, "If—if you'll tell me next time you see one, I'll put it outside for you."

"I'm sorry, but I don't want them *outside* my house, either."

Singer noticed the squished last bite in her hand and dropped it down for Ish. She went back to her work. "I'm sorry, too. It's your house, and it's natural for you to think it's your spider. But it's not. It's just another beautiful thing that lives here."

May let out an angry breath. "I must tell you—I've had about all the reverence for life I can take for today." She marched to the bedroom door, gave it a sharp rap, and opened it. "Mr. Bascomb," she said firmly.

There was no answer. Coo went in to make certain his favorite person was still there. He came out wagging his tail peacefully. Harley and Singer watched, their scrub rags dripping in their hands.

"Mr. Bascomb! You will have to speak to me sooner or later." Another silence. May yanked the door shut. With fake calmness she sniffed inside the shiny-clean refrigerator that was standing open, airing, and said, "Now that this is usable, I guess I can go get some basics."

And I guess we can go on scrubbing, Harley thought wearily. He thought of something else. "Hey, May, do you suppose the fridge belongs with the house, or is it Bill's?"

"Oh, I'm sure it goes with the . . ." May's eyes went out of focus. "My husband handled all that, so I never bothered to ask." Her tired shoulders drooped. Harley could see it hadn't occurred to her that she might have to shell out for a fridge and no telling what else right off the bat. But she said, with a jut to her chin, "If it's his, I'll stuff it full of his dirty socks and good riddance." She grabbed her purse and strode out.

When he heard Rosabella start, he asked, "Why didn't she just go in there and make him talk? He's awake—you know he is."

"They're both scared," Singer said in a murmur that even a wide-awake Bill couldn't have heard. "That's what all the blustering is about. Like Ish tearing into Coo yesterday—testing, to see where they stand. To them this is a real war that's going to change the rest of their lives."

"It's May's house. Her folks left it to her."

"Okay, but Bill's lived here forever. It's his home, too."

"Her husband left her," he said, not certain he should be passing on what May had told him. "He's gone to his other family in Japan or somewhere. I forget. He left her two years of savings and took off. So this is all she's got."

Singer gave him that smile he had seen before and couldn't place. "I'm glad you and May ran into each other. She deserves somebody like you to make up for all the hurts in her life."

He wished she wouldn't say nice stuff that he didn't know how to take.

She said, "I'm trying to be friendly, but I rub her the wrong way. And she thinks I'm on Bill's side."

"You are."

"Well, not really. I don't take sides."

"Except for spiders, and eating meat, and letting Bill rest—"

She laughed. "Sure, I take up for things that can't take up for themselves. They ought to be respected." She hesitated before she emptied her pan of dirty water into the sink, as if she hoped the gray spider might by some miracle come climbing out of the drain.

"See what I mean?" he said. "You're"—he fumbled

for the right word—"too *nice* or something. Like you're not even living in the real world."

"Well, I live in my own little version of the world, just like everybody else does," she said. "So it's got to be as beautiful and kind and loving—and nice—as I can make it."

"That's dumb," he said. "You don't get to say what the world's like."

"Sure you do." She gazed at him, smiling patiently, until his memory suddenly lurched back to the moment when he had banged the trunk of the Bimmer in some kind of crazy triumph, somehow able to demand his duffel and let the only life he knew disappear in a haze of dust.

"Now, wait a minute," he demanded, feeling tricked into some kind of detour.

She giggled. "You don't get it, do you, Harley? The world's a mirror."

"See?" he insisted. "You say weird things like that!"

"It reflects what you give it. Life does what it sees you doing—so it makes sense to do good, happy things. Right?"

He slung his rag into the sink. May was right—Singer's high-flying talk wasn't easy to take when they had things like starting their lives over to think about.

He was stomping toward the porch when the bedroom door opened. Bill stood in it, leaning against the jamb. He had pulled on his pants and T-shirt, but his white toes still peeped out of the holes in his socks like little bald heads.

"Bill!" Singer beamed. "You're unwoozed! Can I get you anything? You need help getting to the bathroom?"

Bill braced himself as the dogs jostled him with their happy leaps and nose pokes. "I broke out of that hospital and came home for one express purpose. To go to the bathroom all by myself and piss standing up. So allow me."

Singer laughed. "You got it, Bill. A man's got to do what he's got to do."

Bill's free hand stroked dog heads as he stared around the room. "What happened? Burglars?"

"It's all out in the yard," Singer said. "Would you like coffee?" Her gaze followed his as it passed across the empty cabinets and the counters littered with cleaning supplies. "Well, maybe a nice cup of ammonia? Liquid wax?"

Bill grunted. "I'm about to reach that point. But there's something I need worse right now. Although it galls me considerably to admit it. On my little trip from Freeling this morning, I discovered I would've been a lot better off with a couple of crutches."

"Crutches?" Singer looked worried. "Maybe we can rent you some."

The hint of a smile crinkled Bill's stubbled cheeks. "You ought to know me better than that, darlin'. Out in the shed, southeast corner, lying across the rafters with fishing rods and quarter round."

"Impressive," Singer said happily. "I'll be back in a flash." The dogs skittered after her. As the back screen door slammed, she yelled from outside, "Oh, Bill—that's Harley."

They were left eyeing each other. Bill said, "Well, that certainly clarified everything."

Harley forced himself to lean casually against the humming refrigerator. One run-in with Bill was all he meant to let himself be pushed into.

"That your dog?" Bill asked.

Harley nodded, startled, still not used to claiming Ish.

Bill's hand left the door frame and slid along the counter to a little pile of trash May had pushed together. His shaky fingers stirred it and picked out two screws and a pencil three inches long. He put them grimly into his pocket.

Harley's pose grew even stiffer as he struggled to decide who he ought to be with this strange old guy. "What's quarter round?" he asked.

Without moving from the doorway, Bill ran his hand up and down the long narrow strip of wood that trimmed it. "Molding."

"Oh." He glanced out into the backyard. Singer and the dogs had disappeared. "How come you have crutches out there?"

"The price was right," Bill said. "Fifty cents apiece. Flea market, back in 1966."

"And you still remember where they are?"

"A thing won't do you any good if you don't know you've got it."

They both looked around uneasily at the emptied

shelves and drawers. It's funny, Harley thought. I sort of know him already—from all the things he's collected and likes having around.

To break the silence he said, "So nobody's going to come from the hospital and try to take you back?" In movies they always did—two guys with a little truck and a straitjacket.

Bill shook his head. "Oh, they may send me a sassy letter saying they can't be responsible because I left without being dismissed. Discharged, discarded. Whatever they call it. But I warned them from the minute they stuffed me in that bed: 'You turn your back and I'm out of here.' "

Harley swallowed a grin, thinking of the bedpan blazing merrily. He wanted to ask Bill what he had made a fire with. Surely not get-well cards—who'd know to send any, or want to?

"They're glad to be rid of me," Bill said. He fanned his hand stiffly at the room. "Where'd she go? I heard her drive off. Has she gone to sic the sheriff on me?"

"To get groceries. Now that the fridge is clean, she's going to restock."

"Not my refrigerator, she's not."

"Oh, man," Harley sighed. "It *is* yours?"

"You bet it is: 1982. Thirty-five dollars and two snow tires. It's a good one. I've got the receipt there in the—" Bill stopped. "I *had* the receipt till the cyclone blasted through my kitchen."

His description of May surprised a disloyal smile out of Harley. "Singer told her the trash ought to go behind the shed to be picked up. That way you can go back there and look through it. Without her knowing."

"Well, bless her heart," Bill said. "But I don't have trash service."

"Yeah, Singer told me." Not that I couldn't tell, he nearly added.

Suddenly Bill coughed. When he straightened up, his face was pale. "Big mistake," he gasped, breathing raggedly. "Got to lie back down. Can't wait for the crutches." His shaky hand grabbed Harley's arm.

Harley went stiff. He'd hated when Vernie yelled for him to help her get to bed after some guy left her smashed at the door. But he took a deep gulp of air and guided Bill back to the bedroom. Get *in* here! he ordered Singer silently. What do I do?

"Looks like I overdid it this morning." Bill's drawn face relaxed a little as Harley eased him down onto the bed. "Dang, I thought I was better. I hate lying here like leftover potatoes."

Harley had to know something for certain. He gathered all his courage into one full breath. "If you're faking, you might as well give up. She's going to win."

Bill glared at him in silence. Slowly he pulled his T-shirt up to the middle of his chest. With more light in the room, Harley saw that what he had thought was a large tattoo was a black-and-purple bruise. "That's the little one," Bill said. "They told me the ones on my back were the whoppers. So wouldn't you think some of my insides took a beating, too?" He rested a moment. "Now, I'll tell you two things for a fact. Number one, I wish I was faking. Number two, she's not taking over my house without a fight."

———

EIGHT

Singer leaned the old-fashioned wooden crutches against the headboard of Bill's bed and propped her hands on her hips. "Okay," she said sternly, "what's the spilled paint and ladder all about? Were you up on the shed?"

Bill rolled his eyes to the kite flying across the ceiling. "Not up *on* the shed. I was just about to paint my name in big letters on the gable end."

Harley hunted around for a place to sit and listen, but there wasn't any, so he sank to the floor. Singer said, "Your name in big letters," as if Bill had made sense.

Bill sighed. "You want this fast, or good?"

"Fast *and* good."

Bill carefully squirmed himself comfortable on his pillow. "Well, this real estate lady drives up and tells me my landlady in California wants me out of the house. Immediately, if not sooner. Well, that knocked me out so bad, I guess I sent her packing a little quick." Coo came in softly and jumped up onto the bed. Bill smoothed his big droopy head as it bent over him. "Dang, I couldn't leave here. How was I going to find some other place I could afford, where I could take this old guy and all my things?"

Oh, man, how am *I* going to find a place? Harley

wondered, as Ish plopped down beside him. Suddenly Ish laid his muzzle in his lap. Harley flushed with pleasure. He couldn't remember ever being picked out like that to be with.

"The red paint, Bill," Singer said.

"Yes. Well, I was so mad and scared, all I could think to do was to set up my extension ladder and paint BILL BASCOMB as big as I could get it on the end of the shed. To say, 'Listen, you—this is my home!' "

Singer smiled. "I love it, Bill. It's got passion."

"Has it? Well, pretty soon that real estate lady drives up again to finish having it out with me. I look around at her, and the ladder gives a little twist and heads for the ground in a nice cannonball arc, with me riding on it. I think I landed first, then the ladder, then the paint in a big splatter, just before everything went black. I may have looked a lot like a dropped watermelon."

"Or you may have just looked *dead*," Singer said.

"Yes, well, I was lying there waiting for my brain to stop sparking, and she screamed and ran off."

"She just left you?" Harley asked.

"For a couple of minutes. Then back she comes with some total stranger she's stopped in the road. And they stick me in her car, with me yelling I can't go to a hospital till I start getting Medicare. And this poor little guy, he's shoving real estate listings between me and the car seat everywhere I have paint on me."

Singer broke into giggles, seeing it, and then got

serious again. "Bill, you could have killed your crazy self."

He pondered that awhile. "The idea may have been in the back of my mind, darlin'," he said, and scratched under Coo's chin.

Singer stood up and took Bill's knobby hands. "I'm glad you decided against it. You're getting better by the minute, Bill. You are." Harley could almost see her squeezing strength and hopefulness into Bill's fingers through her own.

He tried to think who had ever touched him with that kind of intensity. Nobody had. He heaved himself up. Ish leaped up, too, gazing into his face to see what direction they were going to take.

Bill swept his hand slowly toward the table. "Take those with you. They ought to be in the refrigerator."

Harley leaned over the clutter and gingerly picked up the rest of Mrs. Maloney's collection of bones in their plastic bag. "You sure? May's going to explode when she looks in."

"Then it's lucky you haven't finished cleaning the kitchen," Bill said.

Singer shooed Harley and Ish ahead of her, and gently closed the door. She went back to work. As Harley knelt to clean under the sink, Ish squeezed in, too, happy to be helping.

May came back half an hour later, struggling with a huge sack of groceries. "There's more in Rosabella," she announced with a bright smile. They all went out. In the back, behind more sacks, were three gallons of white paint, surrounded by trays and rollers and brushes.

"No, May," Harley groaned.

"Oh, yes." She actually laughed. "It was half price! We'll do the kitchen and bath, at least, before we put anything back. It'll make all the difference."

"I thought you were broke," Harley said.

She looked him straight in the eye. "I thought I was, too—broke, scared, helpless, and out of my depth. But I'm not! I stored my personal things with my neighbor when I left. I'll ask her to sell the silverware—it was mine from my aunt when I married. And my husband once bought me a fur coat I've always hated." Harley saw her glance at Singer, who beamed back. "So for a few weeks, anyway, I am a wonderful, rich, self-sufficient old woman."

"I love it, May," Singer said.

"So do I," May agreed. "I had forgotten what I promised myself I was going to be. The paint reminded me. Everything new and better." She opened the refrigerator and didn't even flinch, just put the bones in the freezer compartment and stuck frozen orange juice in front of them.

"It's his fridge," Harley said.

"Is it?" Her voice stayed chipper. "Well, right now it's in my kitchen, so I'll put my food in it."

Singer asked, "Want me to do shelf paper so we can set things away?"

"No. I want you to paint, if you're not too tired," May said with a new burst of energy. She turned to Harley. "And I want you to copy whatever she does, because she's more than likely an expert."

He and Singer exchanged dubious glances. How, he wondered, had she decided to handle Bill, who was probably listening from the bedroom, as befuddled as they were?

"Ceiling first. Start here above the sink so we won't be in each other's way later when I start the pizza." She brought two large shiny pizza pans from her sack.

Harley waited for Singer to say, "Hey, I came to help *Bill*—paint your own ceiling." But she smiled and began to lay old newspapers over the countertops.

May tore up more rags to mop dribbles with. "Don't try to do a fancy job—just cover the grime." She was so excited, she seemed to forget she'd barely been on speaking terms with Singer just that morning. She unpacked more groceries. "I got flower and vegetable seeds—it's not too late to start a garden."

"I'll bet Bill's already started one," Singer said, pouring a tray of paint.

May hardly hesitated. "I mean a *real* garden. *Huge.*"

Singer handed Harley a tray and roller. "Try a wall— it's easier. Till you get the hang of it." She got on a stool and took down the ceiling light fixture. Generations of miller moths tumbled out. She made up another tray. "Roll, Harley. Think pizza."

Wearily he copied what she was doing, except he went

up and down the wall while she went back and forth across the ceiling. After the first ten wobbly strokes, his cramped fingers began to ache. He didn't know how Daddy had stood painting for a living, year after year. But this was the bargain. This gave him the pizza, and the bed.

When Coo barked, he gladly stopped and opened Bill's door. "Out!" May ordered, pointing toward the porch with a can of tomato sauce. Coo placidly obeyed, sideswiping the fresh wall and then painting the stove on his way. "Take both of them, before they ruin everything!" she added as Ish lifted his white nose from Harley's tray.

Singer urged them out, following with a wet cloth to use on them. With his foot Harley anxiously slid his own rag over the little trail of ghostly paw prints left behind, hoping May was too busy slashing peppers and onions to notice.

Singer came back in and made a salad. May came up with a chocolate pudding. The day had been so long, and everything smelled so wonderful, he thought he'd collapse before they ate.

They left the stuffy kitchen and carried supper into the yard—where the table was, anyway. He'd never tasted anything so good. May actually smiled, watching him eat. She had left the pepperoni off half of one of the pizzas.

"I didn't know you could make pizza at home," he admitted, balancing his third heavy slice in midair.

"My husband had a youth choir at one time," May said. "We'd have them over. I learned then." For the first time since she'd returned with the groceries, a shadow seemed to cross her face.

The dogs, waiting under the table for manna to fall, suddenly went wagging toward the porch. They all turned, still chewing, and saw Bill standing at the screen door with his crutches.

Singer was up in a flash. "Bill—how was the nap? Do you want to try walking outside a little bit? I'll help you."

From behind a fixed smile, May murmured to Harley, "Glory be, we've had a miraculous healing—brought about by the smell of pizza." She raised her voice. "Will you join us, Mr. Bascomb? There's plenty."

"Thank you, no, ma'am." Bill stopped at the top of the steps. But Singer was already coaxing him down. Slowly he swung himself toward the table as she brought a chair. "I won't interrupt you. I thought a little fresh air—"

"Nonsense," May said pleasantly. One pan had two slices left on it, and she slid it toward him. Singer helped him sit and propped his crutches close by.

"Well, thank you very much," Bill said to the pizza. "It looks as good as it smells."

Singer handed him the fork Harley had bypassed in favor of his fingers. "You're looking good, too, Bill."

"Yes," May agreed. "I hope you had a good, long rest today. And I hope we didn't make too much noise."

Bill finally looked into her face. "No, ma'am, you didn't make too much. Just enough."

A silence dropped. Harley watched Bill's ears wiggle slightly as he chewed. Singer offered Bill the last blob of salad.

"I wasn't sure I had walked into the right kitchen," Bill said.

"It does look—brighter, doesn't it?" May said, looking bright herself.

Bill gazed around at the things in the yard. "You're not putting any of this back in there, I take it."

"No, Mr. Bascomb. I'm letting you truck it away to your new residence. Even the trash in the plastic bags, if you like."

Bill started to give his crust to Coo, but changed his mind and ate it himself. "I don't have a new residence, dear lady. You didn't give me a whole lot of warning before you swooped in here."

"I did explain to the realtor that it was an emergency. She did tell you that, didn't she?" Her voice had lost some of its lightness. "Don't you have a friend or relative you can stay with until you're able to look for a new place?"

As though he were a pizza commercial, they all watched him bite into his second slice. "Don't *you* have a friend or relative," he asked her, "so *you* could stay somewhere and give me my month's notice?" He glanced at her indignant face and added in a calmer voice, "The fact is, I don't have the money for a new place. That would mean the first month's rent and a deposit and somebody to help me move my things. Even without this hospital expense, I don't have it."

"But surely you've got hospitalization insurance," May said.

"No, ma'am. My Social Security starts next year. They tell me it's going to be piddling, but at least it'll give me hospitalization then."

Everything he said seemed to deflate May's airy mood a little more. Harley watched her bristle herself back into control. "Well, the fact remains, you have to give me back my house, Mr. Bascomb."

Bill shrugged. "Well, the fact remains, you're going to have to take it."

Go down slugging, Harley thought before he could stop himself.

May got up with an I-don't-have-to-listen-to-this look. She piled dirty dishes on her new pizza pans and carried them to the kitchen.

"Bill, she was in such a nice picking-herself-up mood," Singer chided gently. "Don't spoil it."

Bill smashed a crumb with his thumb. "I just shared some simple facts of life. Her mood is up to her."

Singer glanced at Harley as though she were wondering if she had the right to say what she was about to. "Somebody's just betrayed her pretty badly, Bill. Someone she trusted. I know that's not your fault, but it might make you a little more lenient with her. Her husband left her. He's had another family somewhere all this time, and now he's gone to live with them."

Bill chased the last of the salad around the bowl. "So I'm supposed to change my life because she came running back here to mope?"

Harley looked away. He had been liking Bill, but suddenly he was hearing Vernie as she cut him down to nothing beside the Bimmer.

May came back for the last of the dishes. "You can surely understand, Mr. Bascomb, that I don't want a strange man spending his nights in my house." Her voice sounded husky, as if she were fighting tears.

"I don't see you upset about sharing the house with two kids a whole lot stranger than I am," Bill said. "But then they're helping you get settled in, and I'm not."

"Singer is here because of *you*, Mr. Bascomb! I'm trying hard to handle this tangle you've caused as best I can. And for your information, the person Harley was expecting to stay with has died. He's having to rethink his living arrangements. Then he'll be on his way."

Harley's pizza-packed insides bunched into a knot. Rethinking? He couldn't rethink Vernie. Or bring back Daddy. Didn't she understand that what she had casually called being "on his way" meant stepping off into a void? He wanted to tell her, What I'm rethinking is, it feels wonderful, all of us sitting here—don't make me leave.

Singer smiled, giving each dog a bit of crust. "Has it struck you what lucky dogs we all are, to have places to sleep tonight? We're going to feel a lot better in the morning."

"I was hoping we might paint a little longer," May said.

Singer shrugged. "If you really want to. But we can't change everything in one day."

Bill fumbled for his crutches and let Singer help him climb the steps to the porch. Harley hesitated beside May in the dark until she said, "Go on in. You're tired. I think I'll just—sit here awhile." Her eyes were fixed on the first bright, lonely star in the west as if she had a wish list as long as her arm.

In his mind he begged her, Make one for me, too.

NINE

Early the next morning, they brought in the table, covered with dewy goose bumps, and had breakfast inside. This time Harley remembered to feed the dogs even though any bowls were as lost as ever. He stood watching as they gobbled their separate piles of kibble, each still wary about getting his share. He had never thought how trustful they had to be, to believe someone like him would come with food every day of their lives.

Harley, Singer, and May were painting when Bill stumped in and discovered they had made rags from his favorite shirt.

May protested she had found it in tatters behind the refrigerator. Bill said that's where he kept it, and then hitched laboriously down the steps to wipe the dew off his car parts and desk and bookcase. Harley sighed. The war was still going strong.

May glared out at Bill. "He's going to do it, isn't he? He's determined to stay right here in my house!"

Singer stopped washing paint rollers in the sink. "He's just out of the hospital, May. He can't haul this houseful of furniture and that shedful of junk away and cram it into a little house trailer or a room somewhere. And that's probably all he can afford. Be patient—it's a hard time."

She gestured at the light, clean room. "Just focus on how wonderful it's going to look."

Oh, absolutely! Harley wanted to tell her. Let's paint the whole house—the bathtub and doorknobs and light fixtures—and then paint the shed and fences, and plant that huge, real garden, and keep finding things to do for years. Focus on needing me, May.

"Well, he's *not* going to thwart me," she said. "I've had all the upheaval I can take." She straightened her rounded old shoulders as if she hadn't heard a word Singer had said, and abruptly turned on her. "What are *you* getting out of this strange situation?"

Singer laughed in surprise and spread her hands. "Pruney fingers?"

For the first time it struck Harley that she was there, making a place for herself, just the way he was. And like him, she would be shown the door when the work was done. What dirty house would she clean next? he wondered. Who would she find to stand up for, with her crazy, determined cheerfulness?

She said, "May, it must be hard to have three extra people wandering around in your life. And to have a yard full of furniture that's going to warp and ruin the first time it rains. Do you suppose you could use some of the stuff Bill's got packed into all these rooms?"

"Absolutely not," May replied.

Harley's brush stopped. She'd sounded exactly like the sister of the little, fat bald-headed guy he and Vernie had been staying with last. The old guy had been kind of nice—he let Vernie drive his car around, and practically take over his house while he was off on business. But his sister had come to check up on things and sized up the situation in a minute. She set Vernie and her clothes out on the sidewalk and fractured her makeup mirror with one big wallop, for bad luck. She had said, "Absolutely not," just like May.

Living there in that guy's house, with Vernie around a lot, had given Harley the best hint he'd ever had of what a home was.

He realized May was saying, "Why don't you two start cleaning the bathroom? We'll paint there next."

He followed Singer and the dogs, already feeling tired. As he lifted down the fake-fur moose head, its bearded chin dropped, startling him with a smiling mouthful of white cloth teeth.

"I love it!" Singer giggled.

He shot her a glance through the moose's rack. She sure said *love* a lot.

She opened a medicine cabinet and began to fill a box with bottles and tubes. "Oh, boy—a prescription from 1962. Worthless. Even dangerous." She pitched it into a new yard-size trash bag. As she emptied the wastebasket in on top of it, she broke into that husky cackle he liked. "Eleven empty toilet paper rolls. Imagine having to wonder eleven times, Don't I need to *save* this for something?" She looked as happy as the moose head he had propped in the bathtub.

He asked, "You think they like all this—this—"

"Bickering?" she finished for him. "Sure, in a way it makes sense. Bill's all shook up because his life's changing. And because his body let him down all of a sudden. So it's a relief to blame it all on May and feel pitiful. People crave a lot of sympathy when they're scared."

"And May?" he asked in a lower voice, remembering she was an eavesdropper.

"Well, she can't very well break her husband's nose or have him arrested—which is what she'd love to do right now, wouldn't you think? But she *can* be mad at Bill and his dirt, because they're both handy."

Something crashed in the kitchen, followed by a little cry. They and both dogs tried to get through the bathroom door at the same time.

May stood at the sink looking down at a dark blob of blood growing on one of her fingers. "Oh, I wasn't calling for help," she exclaimed. "I just broke one of his stupid jelly glasses." She tore a narrow strip from the roll of paper towels she'd bought and wrapped it around the cut.

"It looks really deep, May," Singer said, picking shattered glass from the sink. "Shouldn't I look for a Band-Aid?"

"In this house?" May waved her away. "Please—I don't need coddling." She went to the porch and let herself down on Harley's narrow bed. "Go. Go." She looked sort of shaky and pale, holding her finger up in its fat, red package. Harley had to remind himself she could point that finger at the door anytime and say, Out.

Singer said, "If I can't get you something, we'll go back to work."

"No, no, no," May objected. "I mean go *outside*. Not work. No one is going to work around here while I'm taking time out."

Ish jumped up into his place on the bed and knocked the breath halfway out of her. "Take this thing!" she commanded. "Go on a picnic. Stay for *hours!*"

Harley hauled Ish to the floor.

They backed silently into the kitchen and stuffed something to eat into their pockets. May's eyes were closed as they tiptoed out. Ish tore through the backyard gate and down the road ahead of them, sniffing and wetting everything. Even Coo broke into a trot.

"Look how beautiful the dogs are," Singer exclaimed as if she'd just been given permission to speak again.

Harley studied them, suddenly seeing the highlights flowing along Ish's muscles. "You don't notice the same stuff other people do," he said warily. "Or talk like them."

"Really? Well, it's not like we've been sitting around chatting. What do you want to hear? I like large talk best, but I can do small talk. Like, well, I graduated from high school last week. Now all I've got to do is keep learning things on my own till I'm a hundred." She threw a stick for Ish. He bolted through the weeds as if he were two leaps ahead of a buffalo stampede, and brought it back to her, prancing and teasing in delight as she tried to take it from him. "Do you like school?"

He almost stuffed his hands into the pockets of his shorts before he remembered he was carrying his sandwich there. He hadn't had much use for school, even before his future had bottomed out, there at the lake. "I guess I'll maybe—drop out now. Forget the learning and start earning for a change."

She shrugged. "Well, I hope you'll manage to go on learning everything you can—all your life—from school and books and TV and traveling and just living."

She left the road abruptly and crossed a cattle guard into a pasture, heading toward a thick, winding row of trees. He was glad when Ish rushed up to him, bringing a splintered stick. They tugged at it until it broke in two.

She asked, "Do you miss where you lived?"

Her question caused an evening ocean to surge into his memory, red and silver and so large that the sun sank into it like an orange. But he shrugged. "I don't get to liking anything. Then I don't miss it."

"What about your folks?"

"What about them?" He slashed a weed with his half of Ish's stick. "My mom's probably in Houston by now, with this guy she thinks is going to fix her life for her."

She said, "It's too bad you two don't get along. Maybe that'll change as you learn to understand each other better."

He shot her a glance. Had his voice betrayed that little stupid hope he was still holding on to about that?

"What about your father? Is he dead?"

They had reached the trees. He passed into their sun-and-shadow lace. "To me he is. I mean it's just easier to think he is. If he's not, it's the same difference. He doesn't know about me, and I don't know about him. So . . ."

He followed Coo through some brush to the edge of a creek flowing fussily over a bed of rocks. Coo immediately plopped into it at a deep spot. His loose skin seemed to spread out and hold him afloat in the clear water.

"Any brothers or sisters?" Singer asked.

Ish stopped at the weedy bank, trembling with excitement. He found a spot where he could put his nose to the water, but he sniffed cautiously and backed away.

"Nope," Harley said, realizing he had already told her more than he had intended to. "Do you?"

"There's just my dad." She hesitated. "Actually my mom's around."

"You said she's dead," he reminded her.

"She is. But I mean I feel her. Always close. People don't stop loving you just because they leave." She walked on. Ish scrambled along the bank beside her, keeping up with Coo but afraid to join him. "He must not have been around water much," she said in a different voice.

"Get in, Ish," Harley ordered, shaken a little by what she had just said about her mother. Ish wet his paws, retreated, and ran to catch Coo again, quivering with doubt.

Harley sighed. He took off his shoes and waded in. The water was icy against the calves of his legs, and fast.

He groped his way over rocks that were slicker than they looked.

"Come on," he urged. "See, I can do it." Coo paddled near, found he was in a shallow spot, stood up, and showered Harley with cold spray. "Get out here, Ish!" Harley commanded. It would have meant the world to him if Ish had come bounding out when he called.

He stumbled back the way he'd come, and suddenly pulled Ish in. Ish floundered, sank, rose splashing madly, and clawed his way straight up a steep bank.

"Oh, don't scare him like that, Harley—this is new to him," Singer protested, hurrying to comfort Ish with pats and strokes. He gagged on swallowed water and stood against her leg, shivering a little.

"He'd like it if he'd just *do* it," Harley fumed.

Singer looked around. "How about if I throw a stick over to the other side." She began to search beneath one of the huge old leaning trees.

"How about if you do?" he said in irritation, and waded awkwardly across to the other bank.

Her piece of dry root landed at his feet.

"Ish, stick!" he called, hopeful again. "Come." Ish rushed into the water to the tops of his white socks, stopped and stared regretfully at the bobbing root in front of Harley. "Jeez—you're hopeless," Harley told him.

"Be patient," Singer said, pitching a little slab of bark upstream. As it passed Ish, he bounded two steps farther into the creek and snapped it up. When he rushed back onto land, Singer praised him as if he'd just rescued a baby. Then she shucked off her sandals and waded across to the other side, leaving him leaping and wavering like a sandpiper at the water's edge.

"It's just scary the first time," she called back to him. "Come on. Be brave, you big marshmallow. Harley wants you."

Harley squatted and held out his hands. But it was Coo who drifted over to him like a dog-shaped inner tube, lumbered out, and wet him down again with a hearty shake.

"Okay, I give up," he declared, wiping his face. He started off across a field, his steps heavy with disappointment. A pitiful little yodel of dismay almost brought him to a stop, but he plodded on.

Then he heard a splash, and wheeled around. Ish was coming, his legs thrashing, his neck and head stretched like a periscope to stay above water.

It was so beautiful Harley almost yelled, "Thank you!" at the sky as he broke into a run.

"Love him up!" Singer called in delight. Ish crawled out before Harley could get to the creek to help him, his tail flinging necklaces of water pearls off in long arcs as his whole body wagged in triumph.

Harley bent over him, regretting that he'd walked away so soon, and gave Ish's gleaming black shoulders a clumsy pat. But Singer knelt and hugged Ish, whispering squeaky excited sounds that made him bounce and wiggle and slurp her face in joy.

"You did good!" she told him. She cuddled drippy old Coo next. "And you showed him what swimming is!"

Both dogs shook and showered more drops over them. She backed off with a laugh and chased them up a slope where a whole swath of fuzzy dandelions lost their heads in the confusion and scattered in the sunlight.

He started after them slowly. The sky behind them was the stark, impossible blue that Daddy had adjusted his TV to get. Ish charged back to meet him, still sopping and proud of himself, and Singer sighed happily. "It's great to be shown you're loved that much, isn't it?"

He swallowed and said, "I shouldn't have left him. I did it wrong."

"It'll come. You just don't know how yet." Something in his face made her smile fade. She said matter-of-factly, "You don't know much about love, do you, Harley? You haven't seen much of it in your life."

He bristled, thrown off guard. "I'll bet I've seen a lot more of it than you have."

She shrugged. "You've seen lovemaking, maybe, and X-rated movies and stuff. But I don't mean that. I mean love like when you reach out and care in a really deep, glad way about something. Whether it's somebody, or yourself, or God, or the whole planet."

With anybody else, he would have stiffened up and walked off, certain that he was being put down. But to his surprise, he said flatly, "I know what you mean." He raked through his memories for examples. "Like nights when Vernie didn't come in, and Daddy let me stay at his place. Okay? And like times kids would come by for me on the way to school and he'd ask if they'd had breakfast yet, and they never had—so he kept the pancakes coming."

He realized she was nodding. "That's what I mean, all right."

He gestured recklessly toward the spot where Ish had crossed the creek. "And you, back there, hugging the dogs."

She beamed, surprised and pleased, and he suddenly knew where he had seen that smile before. *Dolphins* had been smiling at him like that, from TV screens and photographs, all his life. The very first one had smiled from a huge tank someplace Daddy had taken him, and as he strained through the railing, it had veered close and let its wet rubber skin glide against his fingers.

She said, "Well, I love you and May and Bill like that, Harley, and want your lives to turn out good."

He flushed, shaken up. Listening to her was like hitching on roller skates behind a truck—one minute you're just tooling along, and the next you're rattling across railroad tracks.

"So you need to start practicing feeling loved, Harley. Feeling cared about and held dear. Okay? Start with Ish." Suddenly she sniffed. He stopped a little distance away and got it, too—a sweet, delicate fragrance on the wind. She looked around. "There it is. Russian olive. Oh, and look, Harley—an old apple tree. Look how beautiful and brave. Some little apples have set!" She pointed them out, her face lifted to the light. The sun shot between her fingers as she stretched her hand, and he was so dazzled he had to look away.

They went on in silence, padding barefooted behind the zigzagging dogs through a fortress of trees. *Held dear.* He clutched at the words. All right. He could handle that. That was his new feeling for Ish. And May's feeling for her house. And Bill's for his junk. It just took practice to see it.

They came to a clearing that overlooked the main road. Singer pointed out the Maloneys' long mobile home in the distance. Two little kids were running around inside a fenced yard, and a puppy was following them.

Singer said, "I envy Juana and Al sometimes. I envy families. People with houses, and each other."

He knew the feeling. Oh, man, he knew.

"Would you like to drop in for a quick visit?" she asked.

"No."

"Maybe later," she said.

"There's not going to be a later," he reminded her. "Well, maybe for you—if they have another baby and hire you to help out again, or something. But I'll be . . ." He didn't know how to finish.

They watched as someone came to the door and beckoned the two little kids in. "It's not a really good idea, anyway," she said. "If we walked along the road from there back to May's, it might not be safe for the dogs without leashes." She started back the way they had come.

He followed, watching the slanted sunlight flick across her back. He had heard of enchanted forests. It seemed magical that Singer had come into his life like an answer to something he hadn't even known to ask for.

The dogs were so far ahead, they suddenly disappeared. "Hey!" he called. Ish rushed back to him, his dangling tongue the size of a canoe paddle. He gazed into Harley's face like a summoned jinni, his smile exposing big bubble-gum-pink jaw muscles.

Harley carefully scratched Ish's lifted chin and eased the worry furrow between the white ear and the black one. You crossed the creek to be with me, he thought again in awe.

"I guess I'd better get him a leash," he said.

She turned and waited for him, grinning. "Who do you think might have one?"

Hesitantly he grinned back. "Bill? Hanging from the third rafter between the tuba and the shrunken heads?"

He went hot with pleasure at her quick cackle of laughter. "Ask him when we get back. Unless they've eaten each other up while we were gone."

"If they have—dibs on the moose head."

All at once he swept everything from his mind, thankful to let go into silliness with her. It felt wonderful after all the tense days. Or maybe he meant tense years.

While they were eating their sandwiches on a fallen cottonwood, a big, long-tailed bird landed nearby and stalked around in its black-and-white outfit, questioning them like a nosy waiter in a TV skit. She said magpies had a reputation for arguing a lot and collecting all sorts of little trinkets and dumb things. They named it Bill.

The dogs waited for their apple cores, and then finished supper daintily with a salad of grass blades. Finally all of them sat dreamily watching the shadows fade and evening come. It was like a really special movie Harley could feel drawing to its end. He wished he could keep it going, or at least suspend a second of it in a freeze-frame for a souvenir, but like the hurrying creek, it couldn't stop.

Singer said they'd better get on back. They returned to the spot where they had crossed before, and this time Harley quietly took Ish's collar and walked beside him through the water with little pats and chirps of praise. Singer waited beside Coo, smiling. They put on their shoes and went back to the war.

TEN

When they went in, Bill was sitting on Harley's bed with three fat trash sacks at his feet. Coo jumped up and settled beside him on the covers, muddy and tired and content.

Surprised by the switch in occupants, Harley asked where May was. Bill said he believed she was conducting a test to see how long the human body could lie in bathwater without disintegrating. He had come out to the porch when he first heard water running, over an hour ago.

Singer grinned and hurried off. Harley heard her call through the bathroom door to make sure May hadn't drowned. She came back, smiling, to say May was out of the tub, and on her way to bed. Feeling much better. And glad they had a nice picnic.

"You've been going through the stuff she's trying to throw out, haven't you, Bill?" She punched one of the plastic bags with her toe.

Bill reached into it and held up something gray and crumpled in the dim light. "My perfectly good underpants. And look at this. Letters. My *mail*." He held up a little packet of something lumpy and dark. "Even my prunes."

She said gently, "I think those used to be apricots,

Bill. We'll get you some fresher ones. Even dried, you can't just hoard them, you know—they have to be used. Have you had some supper?"

"I don't want supper."

"How about a peanut butter sandwich? That's what we took on our picnic. I'm going to make you one."

She was gone before he could answer, so he turned to Harley. "I gather you've explored the creek."

"Yeah." He gave Ish's head a proud pat. "We taught Ish how to swim."

Bill clicked his fingers, and Ish came shyly through the trash bags to stand between his feet. "How come you hadn't already taught him?"

"I just got him," Harley said. "Four days ago. The same time I met May, out in this, like, campground in Arizona. A couple of guys just dumped him and drove off."

Bill's hand stopped its sweep across Ish's shoulders and ribs. "Did they, now. Just left you, little guy?" He lifted Ish's muzzle and looked quietly into his face a moment. "So you two sort of . . ."

"Yeah. Like, adopted each other that night."

"And then she adopted both of you—was that it?"

"I guess," Harley said.

"Well, maybe whoever owned him had to move to a new place that wouldn't take dogs. Or maybe couldn't afford the extra insurance."

"Insurance?"

"Well, I don't know about Arizona, but some places get strict about pit bulls and make you carry more."

"Pit bulls?" Harley asked. "He's a pit bull?"

"Maybe not full blood, but really close," Bill said.

Harley looked at Ish as if he had changed color. "I thought pit bulls—" All he'd heard began to jumble in his head. "Aren't they mean? Like—like attacking little kids and all that?"

Bill went back to checking trash bags. "Certain ones are, if all they're taught is how to fight. But if any dog is treated right and has somebody to help him know when he's on the right track, you can arrive at something as sweet as old Coo here, munching his soybean dinner and shedding more love than hairs."

"Oh, man," Harley murmured. "A pit bull. How'd I get into this?" He slid down the wall to the floor and sat holding his knees tight. He could feel the afternoon's lightness seeping away. Singer came from the kitchen balancing three stacked glasses, a tinkling pitcher, and Bill's sandwich. He took the glass she handed him.

"Really a pit bull?" she asked, smiling. "How about if we don't tell him. He's macho enough without trying to live up to a reputation."

"It's not funny," he said, drinking whatever she had given him without tasting it. "I don't need a pit bull— I've got enough troubles already." He could feel Ish's intense eyes on him, full of secrets.

She hesitated a moment. "Maybe you're not ready for a dog, period, Harley. For the give and take of it. No matter what kind." Bill nodded as she went on: "It's a real undertaking, just to feed and exercise and train one, and keep him safe and healthy, with his shots and tags . . ."

Bill said, "He'll be looking up to you and trying to please you. Saying he's an unpopular breed, or old or sick or too much trouble, doesn't give you an excuse to discard him. So if you're not ready for that kind of responsibility, give him up right now. It's not fair to have him."

"But I already have him," Harley said faintly. He gazed at Ish, sitting alertly between Bill's feet. We've already picked each other, he thought. It's too late.

Singer refilled their glasses and sat on the floor with her back against the bed. Ish nosed her arm upward to hint that she could be scratching him. She smiled tiredly and combed his back with her fingernails. Loose white hairs from his neck scattered across his dark coat like Chinese writing on a little blackboard.

"Dang," Bill said, licking his thumb, "that was good, darlin', but I hate to be eating her food."

"She's keeping it in your refrigerator," Singer reminded him with a grin. "And she's sleeping on your sheets."

"On my *bed*," Bill corrected her. "I got that nice mattress and springs for fixing an old boy's fence."

"Then eat, drink, and be thankful for all gifts." She lifted her glass and clinked it with Bill's. Harley gloomily emptied his own glass again.

Bill told him, "Buck up, Harley. You've got a perfectly good, strong, bighearted young dog. You're lucky."

"Oh, you should have seen Ish run on the picnic, Bill," Singer said. "He just about exploded, he was so happy."

"Well, he had a good upbringing, seems like," Bill went on. "Somebody cared enough to have him neutered. Too bad they had his ears cropped, but it was done by a good vet. It's this last bunch that didn't care much for him." His hands roamed over Ish's neck and chest again. "All these little scabs are recent. And he must've tried to get away—his collar's been tightened a couple of holes. It's too tight." He turned to Harley. "You want to loosen it?"

Harley crawled over to the bed and made space between Ish and the trash sacks. He worked the collar loose and buckled it two holes larger. It must have been hurting a long time, and he hadn't even noticed.

"Looks like they kept him tied up, or indoors," Bill said. "His toenails haven't had a chance to wear down." He set his glass on the floor. Ish took a taste from it and snorted in disdain. "I hope I still have some clippers—they *used* to be in a drawer in the kitchen."

Harley listened in silence, smoothing one of Ish's delicate feet. He realized that two other hands besides his were giving Ish small strokes of acceptance and trust. But how was that going to help?

He went out and stood in the gathering dark, feeling heavy and confused. Ish popped through the dog door and drained himself against Bill's desk, sitting out in the middle of the yard, before Harley could stop him. Then he raised his nose to the wind the way all dogs had done since their beginning and confidently identified some scent that humans couldn't even smell.

"What am I going to do with you?" he whispered.

The porch was empty when they went back in. Ish took Coo's damp spot on the bed. Harley sat down tiredly beside him. "Don't do that," he begged as Ish's tail whacked the cover. "We better not get to liking each other so much. Nobody's going to want you—or me, either, if I've got you."

The distracted pats he was giving Ish were more like little shoves, but Ish braced himself and gave Harley's arm a lick. Even that simple thing was too much to bear, and with a moan he hauled Ish tight against his chest.

ELEVEN

The next morning the moose head had to go so Harley and Singer could paint the bathroom. The only open space they could find for it was at the head of Bill's bed, where it hung like an avalanche about to happen.

May said, "I can't bear to step from a bright, clean room into one that looks like the inside of a vacuum cleaner bag." She went into Freeling and bought paint for the rest of the house.

They painted the harsh green walls of her bedroom a pale blue. May thought the cowboy hat on her lamp would make more sense on the moose. It didn't, but Harley stood inside Bill's doorway a long time, trying to imagine having a weird, wonderful room like that.

He was working harder than he had ever worked in his life. But the tiredness was different from bored tiredness. Being needed as part of a team was new, and so was the little tingle of pride when he walked into a freshly painted room he had helped to transform.

They excavated the washing machine out on the porch, and after that May washed everything she could crumple up and throw into it. Loads of laundry constantly billowed on the three clotheslines like a ship in full sail.

May and Bill kept out of each other's way and hardly spoke. He spent part of each day resting, but more and more often he hobbled out to an old chair behind the shed to rescue his treasures from the trash sacks.

On one of Harley's trips to the clothesline with laundry for Singer to hang, he noticed that the sliding door of the shed was open a few inches. He peered in and saw Bill holding a rubber-tipped cane.

Bill shoved his crutches at Harley and pointed to the rafters. "Stick them up there out of my sight. Twitching along on those things could make you an invalid for life." He tested his weight on the cane, holding his jaw tight, and walked slowly toward the door.

Harley climbed up on a huge crock full of old golf balls and stowed the crutches. From his vantage point, he could see lawn mowers and sawhorses and jacks and old batteries and piles of scabby furniture. A faded tarp covered what had to be the old car that belonged to the fenders and radiator they had moved from the kitchen. Under the windows of one wall was a workbench loaded with tools.

"What were you going to do with all this stuff?" he asked.

Bill looked back grim-faced. "Fix it up. Make it run again. Put the shine back. Give it a second chance."

"I wish you didn't have to move it. But she's going to make you, isn't she?"

"Looks like it. It's her shed." He braced his shoulders. "She's right, though—there's really not but one thing in here worth passing on to anybody. If there *was* anybody."

"The old car?"

Bill almost smiled. "You just don't part with a '31 Model A. It's worth something, even as rusty as it is. A lot more, if I could restore it really slick. If she'd let it sit here, she'd still have room for her precious station wagon, if that's what she's worried about."

"I think she's mostly worried about getting taken advantage of, after what her husband did," Harley said, suddenly wondering whose side he was taking. "Like, she's scared to trust anybody anymore."

"She don't seem worried about taking advantage of you kids. She's sure keeping you busy."

Harley shrugged. "It's room and board."

"And after that?"

A rush of anxiety almost knocked Harley off balance. I don't know, he thought in panic. All he could see was a gray empty space.

May peeked in. "Oh, there you are," she said, and shoved the door open farther, as if she thought they had been hiding. "Good Lord, Harley, get down before you fall. Don't you understand I don't have a speck of insurance if something should happen to you?"

Harley waited long enough to show he didn't like being ordered around, then jumped off the crock. Dust puffed up around him.

May slowly seemed to realize she was standing in the only open pathway, blocking them from going out the door. She turned around nervously, upset a table lamp sitting on a barrel, and caught it as it toppled. "I want to start a garden, Mr. Bascomb. Do you have a shovel I could use?"

Bill said dryly, "I happen to have a nice little Rototiller that'll break up the ground a lot easier than spading it. Pick yourself a spot, and I'll show you how to use it."

"You mean some kind of cultivator? I've never—I'm not mechanical."

Bill lifted his shoulders. "Well, I could show the kids how to run it, but you still wouldn't know how to use it when they're gone."

Harley felt a cold wind cross the back of his neck. *Gone.*

May glanced at Harley and away. "Then—if you'll show me how to use it . . ." She went to the door and pointed. "I would like a garden over there, where those weeds are."

Bill looked past her. "If you mean inside that wire fence, that's *my* garden. Already growing."

May looked closer in amazement, still holding her hand out like a one-armed scarecrow. "Well, if those are tomato plants, they're dying under a ton of thistles and volunteer mustard."

"I happen to like letting it grow the way nature would do it."

"Oh, yes, I've already noticed you let everything grow naturally in your house," May said. "Bugs, mold, rust, mice . . ."

Bill scowled. "I give things a place to be happy in, which is more than you're doing."

Before he could stop himself, Harley said, "Jeez—do you have to argue like this?"

Their heads swiveled toward him. Then Bill nodded toward a corner of the shed. "The cultivator's there behind that stack of tires. You want to get it?"

Harley made himself a pathway, slamming things aside as he went. He located a machine with wheels and plow-like fingers, and hauled it back to Bill.

May said with effort, "I've decided to let you have your thirty days to move, Mr. Bascomb." Harley stared at her, not breathing, as he waited for her to say the extension included him, too. But she said, "And I'm willing to buy certain pieces of your furniture if you'll price them reasonably. The bed I'm using. Two of the couches in the—" She clutched the hoe Bill abruptly thrust at her.

Harley couldn't stand it any longer. "What about me?"

May turned to him, biting her lip. "I have to give Mr. Bascomb reasonable time to move, Harley. But I can't have any more complications right now. Not a boy. Good Lord."

Why not? he wanted to yell at her. If old Nolan cheated you out of kids, here's a chance to have one! But that would be a stupid thing to say; she'd only told him what he'd expected to hear.

Suddenly Bill said, "Dear lady, my conscience is going to bother me if I don't confess something. That furniture in your house doesn't belong to me—it was here when I came. It's legally yours."

May glared at him. "That's a despicable way to get out of moving it, Mr. Ba—"

"Bill," he interrupted. "Maybe so, but think about it. If you don't have any money, or furniture, either, and I clear everything out of that house, you'll be sitting on the floor eating raw macaroni with your fingers."

May's mouth formed a word, but only a sputter came out. She turned on her heel and toppled the lamp again. As she caught it, she gasped, "This—I'll just take it in, too."

Harley waited, flabbergasted, until she was out of hearing. "All that stuff in the house *is* yours, Bill, isn't it? Why did you say it wasn't?"

"Would you just as soon be sleeping on the floor where a daybed used to be?" Bill asked, motioning for Harley to pull the cultivator outside. "She needs furniture. Let it alone."

May came back in, still clutching her new lamp determinedly. "I need a small stepladder. So I can wash the front-porch windows."

"Right behind you," Bill said, rummaging in a box.

She juggled the lamp and ladder, gathering her resolve. "And I accept your gift of the furniture, Mr. Ba—it's possible my husband decided to rent the house furnished. I imagine he was expecting a family."

Bill stuffed a bent straw hat and a pair of cotton work gloves into the crook of her elbow. "Well, he got *me*, May."

"And—and you've never had a family of your own?" she asked. "Children?"

"Are you asking if-I-ever or why-I-never married?" Bill took a heavy rake off a hook on the wall. "Well, I liked my freedom and could stand my cooking, so I figured why bother. And it seems to have saved me some pain, from what I gather, May."

Her chin jutted a little bit, and she said defensively, "It's obvious a woman in your life isn't your primary interest."

Bill actually smiled. "My what? No, ma'am, my primary interest hasn't been women or men or two and a half children and a mortgage. It has happened to be dogs and cats and gardens and tools and old cars and doing as I pleased."

Harley's mouth started to drift open. But he shut it as May said in a tiny voice, "Cats?"

Bill said, "Yes, ma'am. Cats. Among the other joys of my life."

May's voice sank even smaller in wonder. "I love cats, too. I haven't had a cat since I lived in this house. Since high school. I haven't had a cat for nearly fifty years of my life."

To his amazement, Harley heard himself saying, "Old Nolan must not have liked cats any better than he did kids."

"That wasn't necessary, Harley," she said coldly.

"Neither was fifty years without a cat," Bill answered for him. "Get yourself one, May!"

118

She drew herself as tall as she could with her arms loaded, and marched away.

Harley glanced at Bill self-consciously. It was nice to have somebody take his side when he goofed, but judging from the look in May's eyes, he had hurt her. Maybe he had meant to.

They leaned the cultivator, rake, and hoe outside against the shed for her. Bill eased down into his creaky chair and rested his hand on Coo's head.

Singer came around the corner. "Bill, one of the clothesline wires just popped. Lucky it had bath mats on it, and they're dry, but I guess I need to splice it."

Bill nodded at the shed. "Bailing wire on the wall by the window. Pliers in the red box." She smiled and went inside. Bill sighed and drew an old bicycle tube out of one of his treasure sacks. He held it out to Harley. "Tie this to that lowest limb over there."

Harley drew his hand back uncertainly. "What for?"

"To give your dog something to entertain himself with, besides my bath mats."

Harley looked around the shed. "Aw, jeez!" he screeched, seeing what Bill must already have heard. Ish had discovered the broken clothesline and was flinging what was left of a bath mat back and forth so hard that bits of cotton pile floated around him like a blizzard.

Harley rushed to him and grabbed the shreds. Ish delightedly ripped them from his grasp and raced around the yard snowing more fuzz.

"Tell him, 'No!' very firmly," Bill yelled as Harley sprinted after Ish. "Don't use fifty different words. Just 'No,' and look stern, and disappointed in him."

"No," he ordered. Ish pranced away, flourishing the tatters joyfully, his thick neck whisking from side to side. "No!" Harley thundered. "Oh, man. *No!*"

Ish regretfully came to a stop. His head tucked in apprehension. His eyes grew anxious. He laid his scrap of mat on the ground.

Singer was beside Bill by that time. "Now praise!" she called. "It's great you caught him in the act—that's the only way he can make the connections."

Harley sighed and fanned his hand at the worry wrinkles gathered between Ish's ears. "That's a good dog," he murmured. Then he held up the biggest shred. "But you got us in trouble." Ish inched his muzzle toward it to make sure it was his handiwork. It was. He turned away and gazed into space, appalled.

Behind him Singer said, "I'm sorry, Bill. I shouldn't have left the mats on the ground. Ish didn't know—"

"It wasn't your fault," Bill said. He held out the inner tube to Harley again, looking stern. "Get on your toes and clean this mess up—before she comes out the door all bent out of shape and sends you and your ripsnorter friend down the road."

Harley hurried to gather the cotton scraps. Ish sidled up shyly, ready to help, but when he stretched to sniff the tatters and Harley warned, "No!" he quailed and sat down at a distance to repent.

120

"When a dog can't be free to do what comes naturally, you've got to show him what's allowed," Bill told him. "I've got a book. Somewhere."

Harley pressed his mouth tight and carried a double handful of scraps to one of the trash sacks. From behind Bill, Singer signaled to him and went into a little pantomime, putting her hand into her pocket and then holding it out. For once he understood her. "I'll pay for your bath mat," he offered.

Bill thought about it. Then pointedly he said, "Next time."

When the yard was clean enough to keep May from noticing, Singer helped Harley tie the inner tube to a stout limb. When Harley called him, Ish rushed up, feeling so forgiven he gargled a little song.

Harley stretched the inner tube down to him. When Ish felt its rubbery resistance, he suddenly dug his nails into the ground, braced himself, and yanked. He was jerked forward, but immediately backed up, yanked, and braced again. Long taunting growls and little yips of sheer pleasure somehow came out of his clamped mouth. He glanced at Harley to make sure this delight was permitted, and when they all three laughed, he threw himself into the battle with all his passionate heart.

"Play with him, Harley," Singer begged. "Pretend you're going to take it. Say *Grrr* and act silly."

"That's dumb," he said, not about to tell her he didn't know how.

Reluctantly they turned away and went back to their

jobs. Harley took Bill's droplight into the unpainted closet of May's bedroom so he could begin to scrub the walls. As he was washing around the door, he saw a row of faded pencil marks climbing the jamb. He brought the light closer. Beside the lowest mark, someone had printed in crooked letters, OLA MAE, AGE 6. He could make out another one that said, AGE 9. The top one, nearly as high as his head, said, MAY—14.

Suddenly he saw her shooting up tall and expectant, before she began to be squeezed into who she was now, and as his soapy rag lifted to swipe away the marks, he stopped, and left them.

But as he passed her clothes, laid out on her bed to give him room in the closet, he gulped, thinking what if *they* had been hanging on the clothesline instead of bath mats.

TWELVE

Harley waited to be the last to get a bath so Ish could play longer, but finally left him, still clamped to his stretched and frazzled plaything. As he came out of the steamy bathroom in his underwear, he heard Singer call softly, "He's in here." He bundled his dirty clothes self-consciously in front of him and leaned around the living room door.

She was propped up on her couch bed, with a book in her lap and a lopsided old gooseneck lamp on a box behind her. She smiled, pointing to Ish sprawled in the spot where her feet would need to go when she scooted down to sleep. "I guess he came in and couldn't find you," she whispered. "He's one pooped puppy."

"Yeah—Bill sure knew what he'd like." He glanced at May's closed door. When Singer gave Ish a gentle nudge with her toe under the sheet, Harley came and tugged his collar. Ish didn't move. Harley shrugged in mock helplessness. "I was afraid of this," he whispered. "You eat a bath mat and you get this irresistible urge to lie flat and not move."

Singer giggled and popped her hand over her mouth. Ish opened one eye and swiveled his ears like someone turning down an annoying radio. Harley couldn't help giggling, too.

May suddenly opened the door to her room. "What's going on?" she asked suspiciously, tying her robe.

For an instant they froze, startled into silence. Then Singer said, "We didn't mean to wake you up, May."

"Oh, I'm sure you didn't."

"I came for Ish," Harley explained, giving Ish's collar an idiotic little jerk as proof.

May sized him up. "Don't you have pajamas?"

He clutched his clothes bundle tighter. "No," he said.

May took a tired breath. "Then I suggest you ask Mr. Bascomb to lend you some if you intend to wander around my house at night."

Harley hauled Ish off the couch and toward the hall, almost bumping into Bill, who suddenly appeared.

"Oh, Bill, sorry if we—" Singer began.

He waved her to a stop. "There's a cloud coming up. It's about to rain." He turned to Harley. "I need some help getting my desk and bookcase and things back in the house."

May's eyebrows flew up. "Don't you mean *my* things, Mr. Bascomb? I don't have room for them. They're not coming back into the house."

Bill's jaw dropped. "You're not going to stand there and let good stuff get soaked."

"I'm not? You could have thought of that and made arrangements for storing or selling all your things when you knew you had to leave, instead of shifting the burden on to me."

Bill turned from her, scowling. "Harley?"

Harley looked from him to May. He was in a spot.

Singer asked, "How about putting everything on the front porch?"

"No," May said.

"Just for tonight? They shouldn't just ruin, May."

"I'm not making it rain."

Like part of the script, the lightning flashed, close enough to make them cringe. "Harley?" Bill asked impatiently.

May said, "You'd love to make him choose between us, wouldn't you?"

"Dang it, woman," Bill suddenly roared, "I want his help for five minutes. Stop playing games with me. I care about that stuff out there—it's still good and worth saving, just because it's *out* there, no matter who the hell it belongs to!" He brushed Harley aside and headed for the backyard.

"Oh, Bill, wait," Singer scolded, getting up quickly. Her sleepshirt said I MUST BE DREAMING. "You'll just hurt yourself again. Harley and I can do it."

Harley felt his feet start to follow her. He stopped and hung in indecision. Did he have to side with May? He knew that everything depended on staying in her good graces. But she was wrong in this, wasn't she? It scared him that she could say no to something out there that just needed a place to belong.

Suddenly he backed into the hall. He had to risk it. "I'll roll up Rosabella's windows while I'm out, May," he called anxiously, pulling on his jeans.

Singer had already taken the drawers out of the ungainly old desk to make it lighter. They carried it through the gate and around to the front porch. In a thunderclap that set Ish shaking, they pushed it close to the wall, then hurried back for more, past Bill limping along with a drawer.

Rain was spattering down by the time they finished. Harley detoured out to Rosabella and had just sprinted into the house when the big drops became a downpour.

May was gone. Her door was closed. Maybe he'd ruined his chances. He felt a gust of regret. He guessed he had let her down. After all, it was her generosity and her roof that were keeping the rain off *him*.

Bill said stiffly, "Thank you. Both. I hated to call on you."

"Anytime, Bill—you know that," Singer said, crawling into her folded sheet, where Ish had sprawled again.

When Bill clumped out, she turned her tired smile on Harley and pulled a book into her lap. When she opened it to a pencil and piece of paper that had been closed up in it, he realized she'd been writing a letter when he first came in.

"To my dad," she said. "I try to write at least once a month." She looked at the letter a long time. "He doesn't write back. Maybe he can't anymore. I wish they had more time there at the hospital to care for him. I know they're busy, but sometimes I feel like they don't even know he's there anymore."

He could see her toes gently rubbing Ish through the

sheet the way his did sometimes when he needed comfort. With a surge of sympathy, he said, "Anyway, writing letters must be kind of a way to be with him." He was startled when she abruptly swiped at her cheeks, where two tears were sliding.

She made a quick little laugh and blotted the letter with her thumb. "I wish I could *be there*, though. Back when he was stronger, my mom and I begged him to let us come live closer, but he said no, we'd do more good just staying where we were. So I just write."

He wondered if he should bring a strip of toilet paper so she could blow her nose.

"But sometimes I feel so discouraged, working for so many needy people. And missing him." She laughed and banged her cheeks, where tears were sliding again.

He came forward before he could stop and sat on the arm of the couch by Ish. "You okay?" he asked, smoothing Ish's flicking ear with a shaky hand.

"Sure," she said. "I don't do this much. It just all of a sudden seemed hard to keep on expecting good things to happen—expecting and expecting. But I know I have to."

He couldn't think how to help her. Or even how to ease the ache in his own throat. He was used to Miss Positive Thinking keeping everybody boosted. He almost reached out and touched her toes still sliding along Ish's ribs from under the sheet.

She smiled and gently touched the letter. "His name

is Lovey. Lovey Ray Rollins. My mother's name was Luz. That means 'light' in Spanish. I like to think about their names. Love and light. Don't you think that's wonderful?"

He nodded again, helplessly, easing Ish off the couch, and started out. With all his heart he wanted to say, What's wonderful is having you like some kind of miracle in my life. But he couldn't say it—he'd had only a day since the picnic to practice being held dear.

THIRTEEN

Harley had the daybed all to himself when he woke up. He chugged his feet around in the emptiness luxuriously, then raised on his elbow to look into the backyard. He expected to hear the little jerked growls of Ish battling the inner tube. But it hung crooked and rain-soaked in the early light. Nothing stirred.

His heart gave a lurch and began to pound. "Ish," he called as softly as he could. The whole house slept, silent. He was into his clothes in half a minute, checking the kitchen as he yanked his shirt on. "Ish?" Bill's door was open, and Coo raised his sleepy head from behind Bill's shoulder. May's door was still closed. He bent over Singer. "I can't find Ish," he whispered.

She was wide-awake and reaching for her jeans before he could turn away.

He checked the backyard carefully, hardly aware of the wet grass chilling his bare feet. How many hours ago could Ish have nosed through the dog door without his knowing?

"Ish!" he yelled. By now he didn't care who he woke.

He hurried around the side of the house, calling loudly, and saw the open gate. His breath caught. He wanted to be dreaming this.

In the front yard he stopped, trying to think what to

do first. Someone in a van roared past, and a fear like the early morning cold settled over him. What did Ish know about cars and staying out of their way? Unwillingly he started down the driveway, knowing he had to look in the road.

Singer appeared on the front porch. "He's not shut up in a closet or anything." She saw where he was going. Her voice dropped. "You want me to go with you?"

He nodded. They walked in silence to the end of the drive and looked both ways down the empty road. He began to breathe again in tight little gulps.

"We need to look a lot farther each way," Singer said. "Watch for his tracks in the muddy spots." They hurried off in opposite directions.

Harley ran along the weedy roadside, where the gravel didn't hurt his feet so much, yelling and whistling until his throat was raw. Would Ish have remembered that day at the creek and gone back there? Or had some instinct urged him to go and find that first person—the one Bill said must have treated him good?

Far away, at the top of a little rise, he looked back and saw Rosabella turning out of the driveway in the direction Singer had taken. He could barely make out Singer lifting her arm to wave as May passed her. He walked backward, filled with misgiving. Help from May was the last thing he would have expected after last night.

He called one last time and waited, turning heavily in a circle. He had to calm down. Lots of people let their dogs roam and they didn't get hurt or lost. From the end of his eye, he saw something dark tucked in the weeds of the ditch. He walked to it. It was a torn piece of plastic. He gave it a kick in a jumbled mix of relief and anxiety.

He almost shouted, What's the big idea, leaving me here scared stiff while you're probably off having fun!

Finally he started back. The station wagon had turned around. It overtook the dot that was Singer and stopped. She must have gotten in, because Rosabella lurched on and, instead of turning in at the house, bore down on him.

All at once May laid on the horn, and Ish's head popped out the window on the passenger's side as he stood up in Singer's lap.

"Oh, man!" he exclaimed as they stopped beside him. He crawled into the back, where Ish attacked him with jarring kisses and tail lashings. "Where've you been, you big dummy?"

"Tearing into the garbage bags in front of a mobile home," May answered for him. Rosabella jerked back and forth as she turned around in the road.

He couldn't see her face, but her voice had a sharpness that made him uneasy. She hadn't taken time to comb her hair. "The Maloneys'?" he asked Singer, up front. She nodded. "Ish, you idiot!" he exploded. "I ought to—" He wished he could think of something to say to Ish that would pass as a thank-you to May, too.

"Save your breath," Singer said. "If you scold him now, he'll think it's for being glad to see you."

He gathered Ish up thankfully in the curve of his arm,

and Ish's black responding nose punched him in the eye as they settled hot and heavy against each other.

"Did you feed him yesterday?" May asked.

A small knot formed in Harley's stomach. "Maybe I forgot," he said, instantly knowing he had. He stared out the window, humbled.

May turned into the drive and parked under the cottonwood to give Rosabella shade during the day. Instead of opening her door, she continued to hold the steering wheel, sliding her nervous fingers along its curves. "Harley, do you remember the night we both started to take responsibility for our future and our happiness?"

"Sure," he murmured, wondering what she was getting at.

She said, "Well, I'm on my own now. And I'm trying my best to make my life the way I want it." Her words came out icy-edged. "Do you understand what I'm saying?"

Sure I do, he thought. You got right to it. Ish and I've just speeded up our leaving date, haven't we?

May said to the windshield, "I know it's hard for you to remember to be responsible for something that just dropped into your life without warning. But Harley, if a small child—or anyone—had hit Ish to force him away from those sacks, he could have bitten them, and I'd be responsible."

"No, you wouldn't," he protested. "I'll watch him better. He's my dog—I'm responsible for him."

"Harley, I just can't have my life messed up any worse

than it is—by you or anybody." May hitched around in the driver's seat and demanded, "Where have you decided to go? Someone has to take you in, or I'll send you back to your mother. There are limits to what I can take."

He turned from her intense face, making fists to keep his last, thin hopes from sliding through his fingers. With all the bravado he could find, he said, "You're bluffing. You don't know her last name or her address. Just try to send me."

He saw Bill lean out the screen door to check on them. Singer made a tiny victory sign and pointed to Ish. Bill nodded and went back in. But old Coo came out and sat waiting for them with his nose poked through the fence.

"You're letting *Bill* stay," he said, forcing his voice steady. "You could at least let Singer stay—you keep putting her down when she deserves to have something good more than any of us!" He surprised himself, but realized he meant it, from the depths of his heart.

May said, "You don't have the least idea where to go, do you?"

Ish belched and groaned delicately, full of garbage.

"Just—I wanted to stay here with you and Bill and Singer and the dogs. So bad that I never—I don't *want* anyplace else!"

May sighed. "Harley, you deserve security and permanence and self-esteem more than anyone I know. And to be loved, of course. But I've lost all that, too, so how can I be the person to give it to you?"

"Okay, so you can't," he yelled at her. He could feel

all his pretended courage escaping in his voice. "Just forget it—we can manage, better than you can. You're so hot to live without anybody—okay! Ish and I'd rather sleep in a culvert and eat from Dumpsters than clutter up your damn life!"

As if he had just heard his cue in a trained-dog act, Ish stood up stiffly beside Harley, thrust out his muzzle, and threw up with a quick *"Caaak!"* over Rosabella's spotless blue upholstery.

"Oh, damn—don't do that!" Harley yelled, and gave Ish a swat that knocked him off the seat.

"Harley—don't!" Singer exclaimed. She scrambled around on her knees to grab for his hand.

"Get him out," May ordered.

Ish righted himself and heaved again. The rest of his roadside feast erupted over the carpeting and Harley's bare feet. The sudden gush of warm slime made his own insides retch.

"Out!" May shouted. "Oh, good Lord."

Harley yanked the door open and spilled to the ground, dragging Ish with him. As Ish gave a joyful leap of freedom, he hit him again, still holding to his collar. Beyond the surprised yip of pain, he heard May calling, "Oh, get rags. Paper towels!"

He staggered to his feet and felt Singer beside him, catching his hand as he swung again.

He broke from her grasp and ran. Ish skittered out of his way, then wheeled back, jumping up on him in forgiveness. Harley's knee shot out and struck him in the chest.

"Stop that!" May commanded. "Get back here. Have you gone crazy?"

He ran on. There hadn't been even a yelp that time. Just Ish's trusting face coming toward him, and then a kind of *thunk*.

Out of sight behind the shed, he stopped, gulping air while his head roared. He slid down against the splintery wall near Bill's trash sacks and drew his knees up tight. Oh, God. What had come over him?

He waited, watching the corner of the shed. He heard the porch screen door open and close. He should go back. Singer was cleaning Rosabella. He should be helping. He wasn't fit to have a dog. Or a friend or anything.

The bitter smell of burned toast came from the kitchen. Bill must have started breakfast. He held his knees tighter. He couldn't ever go back in there.

Finally he heard Rosabella's door shut. Singer had finished. In a daze of anxiety, he scraped vomit off his feet with a little chip of wood.

When he lifted his head, she was standing at the corner of the shed, drying her hands on her shirtfront. Her face was sad. Ish stood beside her, pressed against her leg. Harley could see little tremors shaking his shoulders.

"I took it out on Ish instead of her," he blurted out. "He didn't deserve that. I hurt him because I let her get me all upset and scared."

"You can't help having a lot of anger in you, Harley, but you can handle it better."

"I don't know how to do it right! I wanted him to love me and trust me, and then I ruined it." His fingers ached to stroke the little shivers away.

"No you didn't—just damaged it some." She gave Ish a gentle nudge toward him, but Ish braced and backed against her leg, dipping his muzzle in apprehension. "Help him, Harley," she said. "Show him things are all right."

He motioned her away with his hand. Even at that small, quick gesture, Ish flinched, and his quivers came faster. "Stick him in the yard," he said.

She hesitated, looking grieved, then took Ish's collar and led him off.

Harley watched them go, amazed that they could walk out of his bad dream and leave him still in it. When he peered around the corner of the shed a few minutes later, Ish was sitting by the inner tube. The tip of his tail moved in a little thump when he saw Harley, but he stayed where he was.

Harley went numbly to the spigot by Bill's garden and washed his feet. When he straightened up, Bill was leaning on the fence nearby.

"How about some breakfast?" Bill asked. Harley shook his head. "Well, then," Bill went on, "May wants to drive you over to the Maloneys' so you can clean up the mess Ish made."

He felt his mouth sag open. "What? No. I'm not

going anywhere with her." His stomach began to knot in anxiety, and he backed away along the fence. "Just leave me alone, okay? It was your stuff we were carrying in out of the rain—why didn't *you* shut the gate?"

"I should have," Bill said. "But right now, from what I gather, you're expected to keep a promise you made to be responsible for Ish."

"Not with her!" He lunged a little farther along the fence. He couldn't just stand there. He couldn't go into the house. And he couldn't get into Rosabella beside May and go back to scrape up garbage while she stared out at him.

"Think about it, Harley," Bill called. He sounded disappointed. So, okay, Harley wanted to tell him, I've disappointed everybody else I care about—let's make it unanimous. He swerved around the end of Bill's garden, tucked his head, and began to run across the rough field beyond May's house. He heard Bill call, "Dang it, what are you doing?"

Oh, man, he thought, crashing through the weeds, I don't *know* what I'm doing—but I'm doing it barefooted. He glanced back and caught a glimpse of Ish springing to his feet on the far side of the yard, his ears cocked in alarm. He wished he hadn't looked back. He had to keep moving. He had to jolt his body and his feelings numb again. He angled out of the field into the road and settled into a steady jog that carried him off in the opposite direction from the Maloneys and their scattered garbage.

He realized it was the direction he had come at dawn,

trembling to think he might find Ish dead. God, what had happened to the thankfulness, the gladness—how had it twisted into this?

His breath suddenly grew ragged, and he slowed to a long marching stride that he could hold.

Then to his horror he heard a car coming, far behind him. He turned, walking backward, but it was a truck— not Rosabella. He turned around in relief and marched on.

It had to overtake him and pull to a stop on the shoulder of the road ahead of him before he recognized it.

He stumbled, thrown out of step by the sight of Bill easing out of the old truck that had been parked behind the shed and limping toward him with his cane. They both stopped and stared across the distance. "I didn't know you were able to drive," Harley said, astonished.

"Neither did I," Bill answered, his face tight with irritation. "Haven't we had enough search-and-rescue for today?" He gestured back toward the truck. "Come over here and get in."

Panic seized Harley, and he started down the road again.

Bill sighed and hobbled along behind him. "Do you know what you're doing, Harley? Are you trying to run away, or what?"

That was stupid. He wouldn't be leaving without Ish. Would he? He edged sharply across the ditch toward the fence of a pasture sweeping off into the distance.

Bill said, "When Ish saw you leaving, he nearly tore down the fence trying to get out and follow you. I thought he was going to bust a gut. So I figured if I could take off after you—"

"Just shut up!" Harley yelled.

"Not until you get in that truck and make up with your dog."

Harley's feet stopped in the ditch. He turned around. Ish was staring at him through the back window of the pickup, his head bobbing up and down as he made little uncertain leaps.

"Jeez—no," Harley groaned. He twisted away and dropped to the ground at the pasture fence. With a quick breath, he slithered under the barbed wire and ran into emptiness.

He heard Bill shouting, "Harley, you're not solving a dang thing, taking off for nowhere!"

He couldn't look back. He dodged through the grabbing brush and weed clumps as grasshoppers shot up around him. He heard the truck's door slam and its engine start. When he looked around, it was swerving back into the road, gunned to the max.

"How *do* I solve it, then?" he yelled at it, and ran on.

When he glanced around a minute later, the pickup was pulling off on the shoulder again several yards farther up the road. He saw Bill get out without his cane and hobble back past the tailgate.

Wrenching apprehension stopped him in his tracks.

Something had happened. Something bad. He had done it.

He watched as Bill knelt in the ditch. With a start he began to walk back toward the fence. He had to know.

"What?" he called, breaking into a run. "What is it?"

FOURTEEN

When Harley reached the fence, he could see the little dark bundle at Bill's feet. "Oh, God," he whispered. He writhed through the barbed wire, hearing his clothes tear.

"He jumped," Bill said in a stunned voice. "I saw that cattle guard up ahead in the fence. I was going to drive through and come after you, you little jackass. But when I pulled out on the road like we were leaving you, he jumped. Right out the window."

Harley stopped ten feet away. Ish was curled up in a little lump. I've killed you, he thought. Then he heard a tiny warble of pain.

"Get over here," Bill ordered. "Help me lift him."

Harley stood planted like one of the fence posts, unable to move. A passing car slowed, and faces stared from it, dreamlike, before it speeded up again.

"Dang it, help me!"

Harley knelt and touched Ish. He could see blood and torn skin. Ish's muzzle twisted back toward his hind leg as if he needed to point to the pain. His eyes cut to Harley's face; then he lowered his head again, trembling.

They scooped their hands under him and carried him as steadily as they could to the pickup.

"Dang, what a pity," Bill panted as they laid him on the seat. "That leg's all to pieces. It's my fault—I was so intent on chasing after you, it never occurred to me he'd jump."

"Is he going to be all right?" Harley asked in a voice he didn't recognize.

"We'll get him to the vet," Bill said, limping around to the driver's side. "Get in, and hold him real still." He climbed grimly into the cab.

Harley positioned himself carefully on the outside edge of the seat to give Ish room. Bill covered Ish with a ragged blue bandanna, and his anxious face peered out from its shadow. I'm sorry, Harley told him silently. Sorry. Sorry.

Bill turned the truck in the clattering gravel and roared off. They sat without speaking. Through his fingers, Harley could feel the regular little shudders of pain. He needed Singer there, giving him her calm, loopy explanation for all this and pouring the kind of healing into Ish that she had passed to Bill as she took his hands that first morning when he came home.

Each time the old truck bumped, he heard Bill mutter, knowing how it must be hurting Ish. They whipped past May's and the Maloneys'. Bill didn't even slow down for Gattman. Finally they saw Freeling ahead. Ish moved, bewildered, and licked Harley's hand. Oh, don't do that! he begged. His stomach knotted. He smoothed the crease between Ish's staring eyes with his thumb.

Bill plowed through the traffic of town and veered into a parking lot at a mall. The sign on a storefront said ANIMAL CLINIC, and a woman with a white cat in her arms was coming out the door. "Let's get him in," Bill said. He got out stiffly and came around to the other door.

You're going out of my life, aren't you, Ish? Harley thought, rigid with dread. Bill had to almost yank him out the door so he could reach in and gather Ish into his arms. Harley stumbled ahead and opened the glass door to the clinic, startled by his pale, warped reflection in it.

A woman hurried from behind a tall counter and led Bill down a corridor. Harley was following when a fog began to swirl around him and he had to put his unsteady hand against the wall to keep it from toppling over on him. A whirring filled his head.

"I can't go," he mumbled. "I'm about to throw up."

Bill turned and hesitated. "Sit down. It's okay." He was directed by the woman into a room, and its door closed.

Harley found a chair and sat gripping its plastic arms. His nausea came and went, sliding like a green wave. I can't even do this right—what's the matter with me! What was I running from when I took off across that pasture?

From somewhere the woman handed him a cup of water on her way to answer her phone. He held it a long time, watching its surface quiver, knowing it wouldn't go down his constricted throat.

He squeezed his burning eyes shut and tried not to breathe the hospital smell. He had been maybe five, he guessed. Before Daddy, anyway. The girl Vernie had left him with wouldn't carry him into the emergency room because she was dressed nice, so he had walked on his cut foot, making stencils down the hall. While they were waiting she had said, "You cry and they'll stitch your mouth shut, too, while they're at it," so he never had.

"Better?" the woman asked him, passing with some papers. He stared after her, too dazed to ask where Ish was.

When he looked around, Bill was limping down the corridor. Harley's heart jumped and began to race. It had only been a few minutes—it was too soon. Bill's face looked drawn. He was going to say, He's too broken up to mend, Harley. Come and tell him good-bye.

Bill saw him, and a look of relief slowly lifted his face. He sat down in the next chair while Harley stared at him, unable to form words into a question.

"He's sedated now," Bill told him. "Not in pain. But he's in what they call shock."

Harley wet his lips so they would work. "Can they fix him up? Is he going to be okay?"

"Well, they'll have to take some X rays once he's stabilized. Then they can tell definitely about the damage."

"But he's going to make it?" Harley asked, sensing the hope in Bill's calmness. "He'll be all right?" He drew a raw breath. "I should've gone in and been with him. So he'd know I was here."

Bill unexpectedly laid his hand on Harley's knee. "You

know I wouldn't have let him get hurt for the world, don't you?" he asked. "I feel really bad about it, Harley."

For the first time, Harley's voice broke. "It's not your fault. He just wanted to come with me when I took off."

He dabbed some water from the cup onto his forehead. Bill said, "You look a little green around the gills. Let's get some air."

He followed queasily as Bill got his cane from the pickup and stumped off along the covered sidewalk. It didn't seem right to leave Ish alone in that ugly building.

"There's something they want you to make a decision about, Harley," Bill said carefully. "Ish's leg—they don't think there's any way they can put a pin in it or anything like that and get it to mend. They say it'll very likely have to go."

"Go?" Harley asked in sudden apprehension. "Like— amputate it?"

Bill nodded.

"No!" he shouted. "He'd *hate* that! He'd hate *me*."

"Harley, it's not that awful. You're thinking in terms of two legs—"

"No—I don't want a tripod dog! He'd be miserable."

"That's stupid, Harley. With three legs he can run and jump and lead a perfectly normal life. The vet says so, and I've seen cases myself."

"Oh, jeez, no," Harley moaned. His stomach churned. "He doesn't deserve that."

"I know. It's hard. But they need for you to decide, so they'll know how to proceed."

"Proceed? What's that mean?"

"Well, they'd do a fine job, I think, Harley. But it's going to cost a bunch of money. So they said after you consider the financial aspect of it, you might decide"—he scowled and rubbed his face—"that he ought to just be put to sleep."

Harley stared at him. He couldn't have heard right. What was to consider? This was Ish they were talking about. He clamped his cold hands to his stomach. "I don't have much money," he whispered. He'd never had to think about the stuff. "My forty dollars?"

Bill smiled sadly. "Ten times that, at the very minimum."

Through his queasiness he said, "I'll pay for it. I'll figure out how. Whatever it takes."

Bill's eyes swerved away regretfully. "You might ought to think carefully about what all this means. You're not exactly in a permanent kind of situation as it stands right now. Maybe if you waited to have a dog till you have a real place to—"

"No," Harley said.

"There are thousands of homeless dogs out there, Harley. You could do four hundred dollars' worth of good—"

"No!" he yelled. "What kind of stupid choice is that?"

Bill looked around the mall and sighed. "I could help out a little bit. I wish I could pay for all of it, but . . ."

Harley crushed his hands into fists. He knew Bill had his own problems and his own dog to think about, but the aching sadness that had seized him by the lake in

Arizona rushed back just the same. Why was I out there, of all the places in the world that evening? he asked himself. Why did I see you, Ish, tearing down that road after somebody who didn't want you?

I want you.

"What'll I do?" he asked.

"Play God," Bill said. "It can be a heartbreaker. I'll be having to do it pretty soon, when Coo's so old he's in pain and not living good anymore, just existing. I'll have to say when it's time. . . ." He stopped at the end of a row of stores. "You get to loving them so much. And then they rush through their little, short lives and leave you to deal with it."

Harley said softly, "I wish Singer was here."

Bill nodded. "I expect she's wondering why we haven't come back." He bent stiffly to pick up a short bolt that had fallen off of something, and dropped it into his pocket, making a little smile. "Once she was telling me this theory about animals that she'd heard somewhere. She believes they help us out. I mean, like our pets especially—they sort of buffer our pain. We stroke it off on them, or sometimes even take it out on them. And they let us. She says look into their eyes. Cattle. Lambs. All the creatures in zoos. Because there's some kind of amazing love we don't understand yet that they're willing to give."

"Why?" Harley asked, gripped by the idea in spite of himself.

"To help us bear being human, she says."

God. What would she say if she were standing there with them, deciding about Ish? he wondered. What would she expect him to say?

"I'm going to try to borrow some money," he told Bill suddenly. "I can at least try to." He took a deep, scared breath. "It'll take some phone calls."

Bill slowly pulled a heap of change from his pocket and slid it into Harley's hand, removing the bolt that had come along with it.

I've got to do this, Ish, Harley explained inside his head. Swallow my pride and ask Vernie to help me help you.

FIFTEEN

"Pinkie?" Harley gulped. He had heard a voice he knew, and his throat had closed up in panic. Finally he could say, "My name's Harley Nunn. I used to come in sometimes with my mom, Vernie. Lavern. She said she'd tell you where she was, so if I needed to get a message to her—"

"Wait just a minute, sugar," Pinkie interrupted busily above the café noise. "She might still be here."

The sudden silence roared in his ears. *Here?* Had he heard right? He waited. He could see Bill studying the tools in the window of a hardware store, far enough away not to seem nosy. Suddenly the receiver was jerked up again.

Vernie's voice said, "Harley? You're lucky you caught us. We're just finishing breakfast. Hey, how are you? I was wondering when you'd call."

He could nearly see her, taut and impatient, still holding her coffee cup. It didn't seem real. "I thought you were in Houston. What are you doing at Pinkie's?"

"We were practically going out the door. Lance was getting his toothpick."

"Lance?" he asked. Something didn't feel right. "I thought he was going to set you up in Houston."

"What?" There was a silence. "Oh, you mean the guy

with the BMW? That sort of fell through. In fact, he had just fired Lance the day he—the day I wised up and left him flat. So Lance and I came back to the coast together. On his bike. You know what motorcycles do to me, babe."

"Yeah," he murmured.

"So here we are," she said. "I can't get over how good everything's going. We're on our way up to Vancouver. You would've missed us if you'd called tonight."

"Yeah?" He steadied his voice carefully. "I was wondering, since things are going good for you, if maybe you could—"

"Oh, going so great I have to pinch myself," Vernie said. "Remember the little, fat bald-headed guy? Lance and I have been staying at his place. Only, day before yesterday he had some kind of heart attack or something. Just all of a sudden, *plop*—flat out in the middle of the floor. And there I was, stepping over him, back and forth, to clean the place up quick so I could call—whatever they are."

"Paramedics?"

"That's it. What a mess. That's why we're leaving."

He said, "So how's he doing?"

"Who knows? They zipped him out of there in a flash, banging on his chest." She was quiet a moment. "So where are you—still in Arizona?"

"No," he said. "I have a dog."

"A *what*? God, that's stupid, Harley. Where are you staying?"

He looked around. Bill was resting against the wall of

the hardware store. "I found some friends," he said, startled as the words came out.

"Hey, I knew you could do it." She laughed quickly. "But you could use some money, is that what you're saying?"

He couldn't keep his voice level. "I wouldn't ask, but my dog—"

"How much? I'm broke right now—I needed a leather jacket for the bike—but the old guy's got stuff he's never going to use, even if he makes it. I could still get at it, before his sister gets here. How much, babe?"

How *much?* He eased the receiver from his ear and looked at it, struck dumb. He couldn't take that kind of money. There had to be better ways.

He said, "I didn't mean I was asking for anything. I was just asking—I mean, wondering—how you're doing."

"Me? I couldn't be better. This guy's such a hunk, Harley. And I think he's got a condo up there in Canada. I'll send Pinkie the address for you."

"Right," he said. Slowly a sorrow with no name filled the place where he had kept his little rags of hope hidden. She wasn't going to change. She didn't want to, or know how.

"And they're treating you good, your friends?" she asked. "Is it a family?"

He thought about it. "Yeah," he said, surprising himself. "A family."

"Well, then wish me as much luck as you're having."

"I do," he said. Meaning it, in spite of everything. He could hear Bill slowly clumping toward him. "So, I'll see you around, okay?"

"Sure, babe," she agreed. Her cup clinked against something, probably as she put it down, impatient to be out the door. "Take care of yourself." She hung up.

He listened to the buzz of distance between them for a little while, and finally let her go.

He had done it all wrong. He hadn't helped the problem or stood up for Ish, or anything.

Bill came close enough to ask, "Any luck?"

He swallowed the bitterness rising in his throat. "She offered to sell an old guy's stuff while he's in the hospital."

Bill gave a sigh. "I see." He squinted out at the parked cars glinting in the sun. "People don't automatically know how to be good parents, Harley. Turn loose and get on with your life. We're going to manage without her. It's okay."

Suddenly he was saying, "No, it's not okay. I want Ish put to sleep. So tell them to just put him to sleep. It's just easier; it's just better. So tell them." In a spasm of despair, he shoved the leftover change at Bill and pushed him toward the clinic.

Bill said, "You don't have to decide this quick."

"I've decided. Tell them."

"Harley, I think she upset you—"

"No, she didn't—just do it! No more trouble for anybody. No big debt to pay off. Just—he won't be here. Okay?"

"Don't decide this fast," Bill said.

"Do it!"

Bill limped slowly past him. At the door of the clinic, he looked back, then went inside.

Horror swept through Harley. He ran for the door, yanked it open, and grabbed Bill's arm. "No," he gasped. "Wait. That wasn't what I meant. I can't do that to him."

Bill gave him a long stare, and gently pulled his arm free. He went to the woman at the counter. Harley could hear his voice faintly through the thudding of his heart. "We'd like for you to tell the doc that if it's what he has to do, to go ahead with the operation."

Harley closed his eyes. What have I done to you? he asked. I've got to keep you running in my mind, Ish. Panting till your whole face is a big smile. Not hating me. I've got to.

He felt Bill beside him, guiding him by the shoulder toward the door.

Outside, Bill said, "They'll let us know in the morning how it went. If there're not any complications, Ish can come home in a few days."

"He doesn't have a home."

"May's, then." He gave Harley's shoulder a little shake that wasn't angry or impatient. It was more like the small mute cuffs of affection he gave old Coo. "We need to get on back—they'll be worried."

"But I have to look for a job," Harley reminded him.

Bill started him toward the truck. "You've already got a job, working for May. But I officially hire you to help me clear out the shed, after you've done whatever she wants you to do every day. Whatever gets sold, you get half for Ish. How's that, for starters?"

Harley nodded, spent. He's right, he told Vernie in his weary head. I've got more important things to do than grieve for what you and I couldn't be.

They drove home in silence. As Bill opened the gate, Harley abruptly stopped short outside the fence, numbed by the sight of the inner tube hanging in the backyard. Bill looked around at him, and went on into the house. He couldn't follow.

A few minutes later, old Coo came stiffly out the dog door and put his nose through a crack to check on him. "Ish is hurt," he whispered into Coo's soft eyes.

The screen slammed, and Singer came out the gate. He braced for what she would say, but she simply walked right into him and put her arms around him.

He went stiff and backed away, sweeping his hand toward the pasture. "I ran. And look what I did to him."

Her hand reached and gripped his, strong and steadying. She said, "Harley, you've got to look past how it appears to be right now, and see him being well again. He will be."

He shook his head. "That's up to them, now."

"No—no, it's up to him, and you, too," she said intensely. "You don't get it yet. It's a big co-op. Everything cooperates! What you and Ish are believing is just as important as all their surgery and X rays. So let's think miracles here, Harley."

"I can't," he said. "I just—there's no such thing."

"That's dumb to say. When you're a miracle yourself—carrying around those ten trillion cells packed into three pounds inside your skull."

That shook him up a second, but he managed to shrug.

"Harley," she chided, "you get to think! And love, and choose, and take charge of your life, and be a power for good."

"Oh, right. So I choose for Ish not to be hurt. And for May to say, 'I take you in.' "

That didn't stop her. "I know it's hard for you to see it, but May cares about you, Harley. I think she's afraid she might weaken and let you into her life—and that would be a really scary commitment for her to make."

"A month?" he asked. "Like Bill? Is that so scary?"

"How about if she's not thinking in months?"

He walked away, too heavy with changes and hurts to play her question game.

"Come and eat when you feel like it. She made you pizza while we were waiting, all worried."

When he got out of sight around the shed, he dropped into Bill's chair. All his anxiety flooded back. Running, Ish! All well again! he thought desperately. I see you chomping sticks! But what he saw was a cage where a frightened dark lump lay motionless.

It was almost evening when he went in. He sank down on his bed. Singer must have been checking on him all along, because she leaned in from the kitchen and gently closed the door. Later, through the screen, he could make out the first star. I wish . . . , he thought. He wished he could feel a familiar warmth and the rise and fall of breath. Instead of regrets.

Abruptly the kitchen door opened, letting light pour over him. May said, "Harley, I'm so sorry. Will you talk to me?"

He didn't move. Did she mean sorry for Ish? For what happened in Rosabella? For the trouble he had been causing her, and was still causing her? Finally the door closed again.

When he woke, it was early morning, and he reached to give Ish a nudge before he remembered he was there alone. He lay rigid a few minutes, wondering how he could have slept.

He went out into the backyard and untied the inner tube. As he turned to go put it in the shed, he saw that Bill was already at work. The old truck was half full of small boxes he had been able to lift. He was starting to collect the money Ish would need.

Harley leaned in at the opened door, staggered by the size of the job he had bargained for. Bill saw him and looked around, too, without expression.

Finally he said, "Over the years I guess I drifted into thinking this was who I was. All I had to show for my life." He gathered some switches and wiring into a box, started out with it, and decided to put it under the workbench instead. After a while he said, "But you know what? This would make a nice little apartment when it's cleaned out. Put in a bath. A sink and a little fridge and something to cook on. There'd still be room for the bench and tools."

Harley said with a heavy feeling, "You mean, like, for you to live in?"

"For whoever. It would give her a little rent money coming in."

Singer swooped around the corner of the shed, dodging Coo like a bullfighter. She kinked her elbow toward the truck. "Already clearing the way for better things, Bill?"

"Just rewriting my history."

She smiled. "Make it outrageously lurid and grand." She hefted a big box. "Does this go in the truck?" Harley was jolted into action, realizing she had come out early to help Bill before the regular work on the house began. He picked up an even larger box. After all, that's what Bill was paying him for.

When they heard May call that breakfast was ready, Bill gave Harley a questioning glance. He shook his head.

By lunchtime he was desperately hungry, and relieved that May had gone to get groceries in Freeling. They made themselves sandwiches and went back out to clean up some old motors and air compressors to sell.

May saw them when she got back, and came to stand by the truck. She said, "I visited Ish."

Harley went rigid in disbelief. Before he could stop, he exclaimed, "I should have been the first one—not you!"

"I'm not sure he knew me," she said, looking unnerved. "He seemed very disoriented, but that's to be expected. They said it went well."

He felt himself go so shaky he was afraid his knees might buckle. It went well? Gratitude washed over him, until he remembered what that meant. The surgery was done, and could never be taken back. He edged into the shed and steadied himself. He wasn't ready to know how Ish looked, lying in his cage dazed and changed.

When he was calm enough to go out, May was saying, "So the receptionist started telling me about this foster care for pets. I'd like to get involved in that. But I realized what I really wanted was a cat of my own. Permanent."

Bill and Singer lifted a lawn mower into the truck bed. Bill said, "They'd love to hear you say that at the Humane Society."

May glanced uncertainly at Harley. "It seemed—somehow—selfish, or callous, while Ish is having such a hard time, to bring a new pet into the house."

Bill asked, "May, whose house is it?"

Her eyes moved from Bill's vexed face to Singer's smiling one, and on to Harley, who quickly made his face go blank in protection. Gradually her tight mouth relaxed. "I'm glad you feel that way," she said, and went back to Rosabella.

She brought a box from the front seat and set it on the ground. They gathered around it. She opened the top, and a little gray face looked at them.

"Oh, May," Singer breathed, and dropped to her

knees. She picked up the kitten gently and gathered it close under her chin. "Oh, sweet baby," she crooned.

Bill grinned and gave the kitten's head a stroke with his grimy thumb. "Well, May, I think you're getting the hang of it."

May let out a relieved breath. "She's mine. Not a foster one. I'll do that later. She's mine till one or the other of us bites the dust." She smiled, looking proud and shy at the same time. "I've named her Glee."

"Glee?" Singer asked. "Like being happy?"

"Yes." May took the kitten from Singer and set her on the ground. Harley backed numbly out of the way. Glee broke into a frisky caper and found herself staring into the muzzle of old Coo. She froze, then arched up on her little toes and spit, giving him a swipe across the nose before he could lumber to his feet and stalk away in disgust.

Bill gave Coo a sympathetic rub on the cheek as he passed, and May said, as if she had just noticed, "You know, Coo is a remarkably forbearing and accepting dog."

Harley went stiff. And Ish isn't—is that what you mean—he's going to eat your cat in one bite? Then he remembered. What kind of threat was a three-legged dog?

Bill turned away and slowly ran his hand over his treasures piled high in the bed of the pickup. Harley and Singer helped him tie a tarp over the load, and he drove away to the New 'n' Used Warehouse out beyond Freeling.

Singer asked, "What would you like for us to be doing, now, May?"

"This!" May answered. "I can't believe he's actually clearing this shed out." She went in to put up the groceries.

Singer watched, smiling, as the kitten bounded in beside May. "Glee's a really brave little thing, to start a new life on a moment's notice like this. But I guess we're all brave when the time comes."

"You don't get what that kitten represents, do you?" Harley asked her. "May's saying she gets to decide who's welcome here." He began to heave metal fence posts into a clanging pile.

May had a pie ready when Bill drove up in the empty truck. They came in and demolished it. Bill pulled some money from his wallet and put it in an empty pickle jar. He set the jar in the middle of the table. May said, "Oh!" in a bright, uncertain voice. "Do we have another new kitty, Mr. Bascomb?"

Harley's jaw dropped in disbelief. Was Bill giving the junk money to May for household expenses, after he'd promised him half of it to pay the vet? He whirled to protest, and almost knocked a second sheaf of bills out of Bill's outstretched hand.

May said, "If my garden does well, it will help a lot with the groceries. I'm so sad the old orchard is gone. We had wonderful apples and cherries."

Harley proudly stuffed his pay into the bottom of his pocket.

Bill said, "You know, May, you could rent a corner of your land for a couple of mobile homes. If you got power in, and water, Harley and I could put in a septic tank and lay out a leach field. You'd have some steady money coming in."

She looked doubtful. "It sounds expensive. My savings wouldn't . . . Besides, they're so—bare and big."

"Then block them off with a bunch of fruit trees."

The kitten skittered up and captured her ankle. She picked Glee up, looking thoughtful. "But trees are expensive, too."

Harley said, "Besides, why should you bother planting little spindly things that you'll never get to enjoy all big and shady?"

She took the bait. "*Someone* would get to. And even a thirty-year-old tree can be enormous."

"Jeez—how old would *you* be in thirty years?" he asked before he thought.

"Ninety-nine," May said.

Singer shouted, "Go for a hundred, May!"

"No," she said stubbornly. "I think I'd go for a hundred and five. I wouldn't want to look like I was just squeaking by."

Suddenly, as she gazed outside over the kitten's head, Harley could see her then, still planting trees—intent, scraping dirt with her old shaky hands and tromping it firm around the roots—until all of them, smiling at her now, were hidden in May's woods under thick flowering branches.

SIXTEEN

Bill said things would bring more if they were cleaned up and in working order. That had Harley back at the shed early again the next morning. Until noon he and Bill scoured the rust from old grills and vises and cast-iron skillets, then loaded the truck again.

They went in for lunch when May and Singer had finished pruning shrubs. The bent straw hat Bill had found for May was still jammed on her head as she dished up fruit salad. She said, "Mr. Bascomb, if you'll show me how to run that tiller contraption, I'll start my garden while Singer does floors."

Harley scrubbed his scraped knuckles and blackened fingernails at the sink, hoping Singer wouldn't just nod. But she did. He sagged into his chair. He was going to be cleaning the shed and loading the truck all by himself. He barely lifted his head while he ate, then pulled himself to his feet and went back to the job.

After a while he heard Bill yelling instructions to May over the chug of the gasoline engine.

In the middle of the afternoon, he crawled up onto an old console radio to pull pipe down from the rafters, fell off, and nearly cracked both shins on a toilet tank. With a sputter of disgust, he gave up and struck out across the road toward the creek.

He didn't go all the way. It wasn't possible to revisit that happiest day of his life. But he sat down at a distance and looked for a long time at the ribbony row of leaning willows and the place where Ish had crossed the creek. What have I done to your life? he thought.

For the first time, he understood why Daddy had cried when his unraveled mop of a dog had died of old age, and why he kept her little bowl and toys. It was terrible to lose something so innocent it didn't know you had faults.

In his memory he let the little dog lick a bald spot in the icing of his seventh-birthday cake once more, while Daddy laughed. Then in his mind he sent Ish crashing through the brush like a pinball, whole and bursting with joy again. They rushed together, silly with delight, and he went *Grrr*.

He woke with one side of his face sunburned and his heart unhealed. When he sneaked back through the twilight, May was hacking at her garden with a rake, leveling the final section of turned earth.

Bill was clearing the supper dishes off the table. He sternly asked, "Where have you been?"

Harley shrugged, feeling a little guilty but not sorry. "Did you think I'd taken off again?"

"Not with Ish coming back tomorrow. But it's considerate to let somebody know where you're going." Bill waved toward the oven. "Your supper's waiting."

"I'm not hungry." He headed for the porch, wondering where Singer was. Bill blocked him so unexpectedly that they bumped together.

Bill said, "Hold it. I'm your boss, and you walked off the job. Now you can do something in here to make up for it. The dishes."

"Hey, just butt out," he answered, breaking Bill's grip. Bill stepped between him and the door to the porch. He hesitated. If Singer were there, her eyes would be warning him: You're not going to shove an old guy propped on a cane, are you? "It's not my house," he added in a lower voice.

"You eat in it and sleep in it. You don't have to own it to wash the dishes."

"Don't you have a dishwasher piled somewhere in your junk heap?"

"The one I'm talking to will do just fine," Bill said, leaning in the doorway. "You know, Harley, there's a powerful word called *cooperation* I'm not sure you've been properly introduced to yet."

Harley turned away. His insides were churning. He took a deep breath and dumped the pile of dishes into the sink. He turned the water on full force, feeling as limp as the dishrag.

"I can dry," Bill said.

"I don't need you."

"In that case, I'll go help Singer in the shed." He went out the back door. Coo got up, aimed a wide yawn at Harley, and followed Bill.

Harley was calmer by the time he had eaten his own supper and cleaned up after it. When he went out to the porch, he saw a long strip of worn webbing on his bed, with a loop on one end and a swivel fastener on the other. Next to it was a thin book. Even in the near dark, he knew Bill had found him a leash and training manual. They lay there as if to say, You don't believe it, but Ish will need these.

He sat down and wound the leash around the book, slowly filling with regret. I'm sorry for everything, Ish, he said in his heart. I'm sorry, Bill.

He went out to the shed. Bill was loading pipe into the truck, working in the light coming through the sliding door. Singer sat on the floor just inside, sorting hinges. Harley stopped at a distance. "Thanks for the leash. And the book—I'll read it."

"You can give him little, short lessons at first. Heel and sit and stay. They're the main ones," Bill said as if they hadn't argued.

Harley nodded. He awkwardly gave Bill a boost with an extra-long pipe and started in for more stuff. Inside he jolted to a stop. The shed was almost cleared out. And where the old car had been was an empty space.

"What happened?" he breathed, afraid he knew.

Bill came in behind him. "Well, it wasn't doing anybody any good. Or Ish, either." He busily piled old magazines into a box. "So on my first load this morning, I talked to an old boy who's been pestering me to sell it to him for a long time. He came out this afternoon with his car trailer and—off it went."

"But, Bill, you loved that old car."

Bill made a wry face and swept his knobby hand toward the wall. "I've kept the important stuff."

Harley turned to look. The workbench was piled high with tools for carpentry, and fixing cars, and plumbing. Bill's welding equipment stood at the end next to his shovels and ladders.

Humbled, he said, "I'll work extra long tomorrow, Bill."

"I don't think so," Bill replied, smiling. "Not with Ish coming." He finally looked directly at the old car's empty space. But he just rested his hand on Singer's bent head, the way he did with Coo, and said, "Let's tell May to come out of that garden before the birds roost on her hat for the night."

They gave her the good advice, but when Harley woke the next morning, May was either out there again or had spent the night whacking clods with the flat of her rake. Glee was there, too, digging a neat little latrine.

Singer had breakfast started. "Ish is coming!" She beamed.

They sat down. A folded check had been added to the pickle jar. Harley stared at it, unable to look at Bill. But he heard him say, "One more load ought to clear the shed completely, May."

She gave a sigh of relief. "You don't know how much I appreciate it, Mr. Bascomb."

Bill said, "I'll store the things from my bedroom out in the shed today, plus anything in the living room you don't want—and the house is all yours."

We're finished here, Harley thought, feeling a breathtaking drop into emptiness.

"Yes," May said, breaking her toast into four neat squares. She turned to Harley. "Mr. Bascomb said you called your mother. Is it possible she'd like for you to come to where she is?"

"I kind of doubt it," he said levelly. "She's on her way to Canada on a motorcycle with a new guy."

She slumped, then gathered up her resolve for something. "I hope you understand you and Ish are welcome to stay here until he's well. Even as long as Mr. Bascomb, if it takes—"

Harley turned his back, too disheartened to listen. He asked Bill, "Can Ish and I come with you and Coo when you go? I'll keep on working for you, besides a regular job. Anything you say."

Bill chewed a long time, uneasily swirling the coffee in his cup. "Harley, I'll probably be in one room above a mom-and-pop café. You and Ish are the last things I need."

In the silence May abruptly pushed back her plate. "Why are you trying to make me a cold-blooded villain here? Didn't I just say I'm willing—"

"No, you quibbled again, May," Bill told her. "Why can't you just say to us, 'Stay—let's try this. Blessings on it.'"

May studied him, amazed. "I can't do that."

"Why? Why can't we stop all this wrangling and what-belongs-to-who, and just go on living here like a family of friends?"

May's mouth dropped open. "Because it's *my* house. And we're *not* a family. Or even friends. I don't even *like* you, Mr. Bascomb."

"Bill."

She said loudly, "I don't even like you, *Bill*!"

"That shouldn't make any difference," Bill said. "But I'd try to dredge up a little more goodwill and tolerance if you would."

"I am not particularly interested in your goodwill," May said distinctly. "I came here for privacy and peace."

Bill said, "And to hide and suffer and be bitter, too, I bet, May. Think about how it's going to be, living alone. You're going to need a new roof really soon. There's a lot of heavy work involved, keeping things up around here. And I'm wondering if you can fix Rosabella when she conks out."

Harley turned to Bill. "I could help with all that—if you'd show me. Couldn't I?"

Bill met his anxious eyes steadily and said, "It goes without saying that I couldn't do it without you, Harley."

A warmth filled him that he had never known before.

May rose from the table, looking disturbed. Her eyes darted to his face, and away. She said, "Harley, you touched me, the moment I saw you there in the desert, letting go of everything you'd known. Starting over. I knew how you felt. I was rooting for you."

He couldn't see what she was getting at. He looked at Bill, but he was listening intently with a tiny smile.

May said, "But you don't need to live a month here with me and then a month with someone else, being passed around like a collection plate. You need stability and permanence—years of it—and I'm not ready for that, until my problems . . . Look at the mess we've made of these last couple of weeks. I could fail you like everyone else has!"

She turned away so abruptly she nearly tripped over Coo, and went back to her garden.

They followed, when the kitchen was clean, and finished loading the truck. Suddenly the shed was empty.

Singer shouted, "Ta-da!" and swept the last sawdust and trash from the bare floor. But Harley stood in the shed's open door gazing at the dark rain clouds that were building in the west like another range of mountains.

"Buck up, Harley," Bill said softly. "Just a few more hours till you get Ish back."

He eased out the door and stood against the wall. My three-legged dog, he thought, forcing himself to say the words. He could see May on her knees, dribbling seeds from little packets, and Glee behind her, scrambling the rows as she romped.

This could be so wonderful, he thought. Why *can't* you bless it?

Singer came out and leaned against the shed beside him. Her face looked sad as she scanned the horizon, too. "I need to remind you of something, Harley."

"Yeah," he mumbled wearily. "Buck up, Harley. Be glad she gave you more days to stay. Be glad Ish is coming."

"Sure, you should do that," she agreed. "But that's not what I meant. I'm leaving. The work's done here. So I want to go. Today."

"What?" he asked when he could make his mouth move.

"I can't be any more help," she said. Her sweaty face turned to his, strained.

"What do you mean?" he said, as dazed as if lightning had just struck between them. "You can't just walk up and say you're *going*. No!"

"How else could I tell you, Harley? We've finished here. It's time for me to go."

He braced his rigid body against the wall. "No, it's not—it's too soon—too sudden."

"But you knew I just came to help Bill, and sort of stayed to help May." She smiled. "And you. And Ish. And none of you need me anymore."

"But we do," he objected, groping for a way to persuade her. "I do—I can't get through this without you."

She took his hand. "Sure you can. I know you can, or I wouldn't be leaving." He pulled away, but she took his fingers tight into hers again. "I want to go be with my father so bad, Harley. I've waited so long. Let me, and be glad with me."

170

"You said he told you to stay here where you'd do more good."

"But I'm not needed here now. He'll understand that."

"The Maloneys could use you. Somebody around here could—"

She laughed, looking at his hand that somehow was gripping hers instead of the other way around. "No, they're fine. So I'm going where my dad is."

"Why, you're scared he's worse, or what?" He saw Bill come out and rope down the pile of things in the back of the pickup.

"No, it's not that. I just want to be close, and get to know him better."

"Have you told Bill?" She nodded. "And May?"

"No, I need to tell her right now. Because I want to go with Bill when he takes this last load in, and he's about ready."

"Oh, jeez—no," he said in despair. He grabbed at Bill as he passed. "Stop her," he begged. "Can't you persuade her?"

Bill said, "I wish I could, Harley. But looks like she's decided."

"But we've got to go get Ish!" Surely she would wait to share that. "What'll I do?"

"Exactly what you'd do if I was here," she said, smiling. She turned to Bill. "The only place I can catch the bus I need is at that truck stop—you know the one? I'm not sure when—midafternoon sometime. So to be safe, maybe—"

"I'll get you there, darlin'," Bill said. "Tell May."

She walked toward the garden. Harley blocked the impulse to follow. "Where's her dad?" he asked.

Bill shrugged. "She never says."

Oh, God, he thought, is she going to be lost out there in the world? "I'm going with her," he said. "Wherever it is."

Bill said regretfully, "Think it over, Harley. You can't go. She knows what you need, and it's not to go with her." He pulled a tarp out of the truck cab. "That rope's not going to do it—let's tie this sucker over the whole load."

Harley had a corner of the tarp thrust into his hands. Distractedly he helped, trying to watch Singer talking to May at the same time. "Maybe May won't let her go," he said, grabbing for something he'd knocked off the pile. When he glanced over again, Singer was gone. May stood in her garden, looking bewildered.

He dropped everything and hurried into the house. Singer had pulled her little suitcase from under the couch where she'd slept. At the sight of it, he said desperately, "At least I can go to the bus station with you."

She pushed back her stringy hair and got her dirty clothes out of the bathroom hamper. She stuffed them and her writing tablet and comb into her suitcase. "No," she said quietly.

"Why not!"

"Because you're going for Ish, and it's in the opposite direction." She added her sleepshirt from under the couch cushion and closed the lid.

"Please don't do this," he whispered. He wasn't getting through to her. She just kept holding that dolphin smile he loved, and receding out of his life as if she didn't know what leaving was. "Will you come back? Will I ever see you again? I have to."

Suddenly she hugged him fiercely and stepped back, still holding his arms with both hands. Her eyes swam with light. "Harley, I'm never going to leave you. I'm never going to stop caring for you. And I promise to pop into your life at the strangest times. Watch for me." She made a quick laugh. "And give that Ish a whopping hug when he gets back. I love him." The back screen door slammed. "I love you, too, May," she called toward it. Outside, Bill pulled the truck as close as he could get to the front door and tapped the horn. She slowly turned loose of Harley's arms. "Remember on the picnic, what I said about my mom?"

"Not really." He frantically tried to think what she meant as he trailed her out the front door. "I don't understand. What?" He was startled to see rain coming down. Through the fan of the windshield wipers, he could see her getting in beside Coo.

She rolled down her window. "You're going to work out a way to take care of each other," she said, then rolled the window back up. He could see her leaning close to the pane, smiling through tears or rain streaks or both as the old truck jolted down the road.

SEVENTEEN

May was standing on the front porch when he started in. Her face was pale. "You could have told her good-bye," he said.

She studied the clouds. "Let's get Ish before it pours."

He closed his eyes, unable to feel anything further. They put down the backseat in Rosabella to make a flat space, and started toward Freeling. "She's a complete mystery to me," May said. "One minute she's here, and then she's gone."

Harley stared out his rain-streaked window in silence.

As they went through Gattman, she said, "He gave her bus fare from the pickle jar."

Harley shrugged. It had to come from somewhere, with her working for nothing. He said, "Bill sold his old car to help pay for Ish. That's what that check is. He loved that old car."

"Did he?" May asked. They drove the rest of the way without speaking.

At the animal clinic, the receptionist said to just have a seat, but Harley was so nervous, he waited standing up. The printing on the big office window looked like Russian. Then he realized it was meant to be read from the outside.

Without warning May murmured, "Oh, look."

He swung around. Ish was coming down the corridor. A man in a lab coat had him in a sling made from a towel, holding the ends of it above his back to steady him as he hopped along.

Oh, God, Harley thought. It's time. He steadied himself against the wall. To his amazement Ish looked the same. Except where his leg had been, he had a little, round, neat hip with a row of prickly stitches across it. Squares of hair had been shaved off all over his body like a patchwork quilt.

Then Ish saw him. His head lifted in recognition, and he slowly broke into a bucking little sprint.

Harley sank to his knees and caught him close. The man slid the towel from under his belly. Ish's back end gave a wag that threw him out of alignment, and he fell over.

"Oh, jeez—no!" Harley gasped. He tried to help as Ish determinedly pulled himself up and balanced again.

"He's just excited. Give him a few more days," the man said. "You'll need to help him urinate and defecate for a while. Just use a towel or something similar to help him balance. And you'll need to come back a week from Monday to have the stitches out—the flap stitches won't dissolve like the inner ones."

Harley nodded, letting the words flow past, and tried to hold Ish steady as their noses bumped joyfully together. He glanced at May, standing at the receptionist's counter clutching some papers and a pill bottle. She was smiling.

"Is he okay?" he asked the man.

"He's doing fine," the man said, and hooked a leash to Ish's collar. He handed it to Harley. "All set to go."

Harley gave it an uncertain twitch. Ish began to wrench along beside him, his back leg trembling as he struggled to keep his balance.

May came to meet them. "Well, Ish," she said. "The worst is over. Come along." She opened the office door. In the driving rain, she hurriedly let down the tailgate of the station wagon.

They lifted Ish in, and Harley crawled in after him. May took the leash back inside. When she returned, Harley was crawling out. "I forgot to ask how much—I didn't tell them I'd pay them."

"I handled it," May said, closing the tailgate on him. She got in. "I paid a third of the bill, Harley. I'm going to pay the rest over the next two months."

"I don't want you paying for it," he said stiffly.

"I called my neighbor the last time I came into town. She'd had a buyer for my silverware and other things. So the money's on its way, and I wanted to make a special gift to Ish from my fur coat. It seems appropriate, wouldn't you say?"

"I can't take it," he said, moving closer to where Ish lay staring warily around.

"Then call it a loan," she said, backing Rosabella into the street. "And pay it back in whatever way feels right for you."

Buildings began to flash by beyond the rain-washed

176

windows, as jumbled as his emotions. He could feel an old familiar warmth through his damp clothes. Over and over he stroked Ish's jaw and neck and ribs, stopping abruptly where the prickly black row of stitches started.

"Does he know what happened to him, do you think?" he asked the back of May's head.

She pondered awhile, and finally said carefully, "I don't think he knows how to lay blame, or be resentful, if that's what you mean. I think, right now, just to feel himself alive and healing is enough."

He said in a softer voice, "You sound like Singer."

"Good Lord," she said.

He began to cry, openly, not trying to hide the ragged sounds or his wet, crooked face. It didn't hurt as much as he had thought it would. Besides, Ish deserved his tears. And Daddy. And Singer. And he deserved the love they had given him.

Ish strained into a sitting position and poked Harley's face anxiously. He stopped crying and swiped his nose on his shirtfront. Slowly he checked to see if all the wiry stitches on Ish's little sewed-up ham were holding.

"I'm learning some unexpected things," May said suddenly. "From a dog, oddly enough."

She handed Harley a tissue without taking her eyes off the road. He wiped the drops of rain and tears from Ish's back.

She went on, "It's obvious Ish isn't going around terror-stricken that he'll never be the same again. He's already decided that his life is not ruined. Just changed."

Harley gave Ish a long, joyous stroke. "Pretty soon he'll be running as good as ever. Jumping. Bill said he would. Whatever he wants. Did you see him coming down that hall? Hardly wobbling! He's learning like crazy—really fast." After a minute it dawned on him what more she had meant. "And so are we, May."

She was silent, but he thought her shoulders straightened a little bit as she drove through the dwindling rain.

When they turned in at the house, the pickup was back. Bill was still sitting in it, and old Coo sat tall beside him. Then Harley noticed that a fallen limb from the cottonwood was blocking the driveway.

Bill got out and came to Rosabella. Harley opened the door. Bill watched Ish draw himself carefully to his three feet. "Now that's a neat job," he said in admiration.

May said, "She caught her bus, I take it."

"She did," Bill said. He gestured toward the fallen limb. "I'm going to need some help with that thing."

Harley got out. Before he knew it, Ish had come tumbling through the door on his own. May made a bleat of alarm, but Ish righted himself and hitched off like a square wheel. Coo gave him a careful sniffing, almost pricking his nose on the little sharp twists of nylon, and then cleaned his ear with a few welcoming slurps.

"Well, Ish," May said as they watched, "you're determined to be a burden and an inspiration to us, in spite of everything, aren't you?"

Harley went over and hefted the thick end of the broken limb. He and Bill slowly dragged it out of the way.

Bill looked up at the jagged wound in the old tree. "Too bad," he said. "May needs to be planting replacements."

"Do you have a saw?" Harley asked.

"Did you think I'd sell off the important things?" Bill gave the limb a push with his foot. "But I'll tell you, it'll be easier to cut when it's drier."

Harley nodded. "So tomorrow, or next day? I'll take care of it, okay? What about up there—can you tell me how to trim it so it'll heal right?"

"I can," Bill said, and smiled as he got in the pickup. He drove back to the shed so May could pull up and park under the tree.

She got out, barefooted to keep her sandals from getting muddy, and stared up at the glistening leaves. "So, what kind of guardian angel is watching over me?" she asked. "Rosabella could have been squashed if we hadn't left to get Ish."

Harley guided Ish to the back porch. He cupped his hands under Ish's belly, and they laboriously climbed the steps. May slowly followed. Bill was putting out dog food and fresh water. Ish tore into his kibble, swaying and bracing as he leaned forward. Harley sat close, steadying him.

He thought in awe, You're back. You're okay. I've got you to care about as long as we live.

The kitten suddenly romped out of the kitchen. She braked and stared big-eyed at Ish. He stretched his neck and lurched toward her. Harley heard May's breath catch, but she didn't screech. He said, "You want me to make him—"

"No," she said tensely. "They'll have to get along. Let them work it out."

She flinched when a growl came from Ish's throat, but Glee simply bristled herself into a hairbrush with legs and held her ground.

"No, Ish," Harley warned. He calmed his voice. "No." Ish stopped and swayed, reconsidering out of reach of Glee's paw. He tried to reverse, but his back leg buckled. Finally he hauled himself around and hippity-hopped back to Harley. "You did fine, Ish," he whispered, hugging him. Ish gave him a poke in the eye.

May whisked Glee away, but Ish chugged along behind them to show the battle wasn't over. Harley found them in the living room. May was sitting on Singer's couch, smoothing the edge of the cushion.

"I regret that I didn't say good-bye," she murmured. "She just—I was—frankly, she grated on my nerves. Ordinary human beings just aren't that uncomplaining and optimistic and giving."

Harley smiled. Singer was Miss Too-Good-to-Be-True, all right. Busy telling everybody how to be. No. Showing them.

Bill came in, fishing in his pocket, and said, "Nearly forgot." He handed May a folded bit of paper. "She said to give you this. Just as she was running for the bus."

May took it hesitantly and held it in her lap. "I didn't

know about her father until today. It must have been painful, wanting to be with him all these years." She stopped and gazed down at her hands so long that Harley finally realized it might be her wedding ring that she was staring at, and old Nolan and his other family that she was seeing.

She began to cry in silence. Slowly she opened Singer's little packet. Something dark made a tiny, shifting lump in one corner.

"Seeds," Harley told Bill as May gazed down at them. "Different kinds of seeds."

Bill came and stirred them with his fingers. "Not anything I recognize. What do you suppose will grow from these, May?"

She shook her head and went on crying as she put the folded paper in her shirt pocket. "I should have made the effort to know her," she said. "Thanked her—"

"It's okay, May," Harley said anxiously. He came close enough to look down on her bent head. He wished he had thought to give her seeds. Something, for all she'd lost. "Could I—would it help any to practice on me?" he asked before he thought.

She raised her head. "Practice?"

"Being loved," he said.

Her blotchy face grew calm. "Yes. I would like to practice on you, Harley."

She put Glee carefully aside, and stood up. She held out her arms, and Harley walked into them. He could hear the seed packet crinkle as she drew him close. All that scrubbing and painting had given her a grip. He looked over her shoulder, surprised that he was taller than she was.

A lump rose in his throat in spite of all his swallowing. He blurted out, "I know it's hard to have kids, May, so if you can't do it, like Vernie, I'll understand." Her arms tightened in a spasm that made both of them catch their breath.

May slowly let him go. "I'm glad Vernie had you," she said softly. She let her hand touch the spot on his cheek where the little scratch from the night they met had healed. "And I'm going to be glad I had you."

He backed away, still gulping, and just missed stepping on Ish. Bill came across the front porch and said from the door, "Come look at this."

He led them out into the front yard and pointed to the east. A huge double rainbow arched against the dark clouds. Beneath the glorious bow, the leaves of the old cottonwood jiggled in the last burst of sunshine. "Dang, I never get over that," he said. "How raindrops and light come together to make that." He shook his head.

May wiped her nose with a tissue from her pocket. The seed packet crinkled as she put the tissue back. "I keep expecting to hear her laugh," she said. "And see her beaming at us."

All at once Harley remembered what Singer had said on the picnic. *People don't stop loving you just because they leave.* "She's around," he said.

He was afraid it had sounded weird, but Bill looked

down at him and nodded. "One thing's for sure, she came when we needed her. Almost like she'd heard us call for help, and—presto."

May said slowly, "Well, in a way. But when *I* asked for help, I got a teenager and a pit bull."

Harley thought she had started to cry again, but then realized she had giggled. He'd just never heard a giggle come out of her before. Then Bill began to chuckle, and for a few seconds their laughing got so hard, they had to hold on to each other's arms.

He didn't get the joke exactly, but he liked the sound. He eased off toward the house. They followed, and at the front steps Bill said, "Aw, look at that. Forgot the stuff here on the porch. Well, I'll make another load tomorrow."

May said, "Actually, I was thinking, if you move your things out to the shed, Bill, and Harley takes your room, the desk and bookcase ought to go there. He's going to need them, with school starting in a little over two months."

"I am?" Harley asked carefully. He gulped a deep breath and held it.

Behind them, in the house, little Glee on the windowsill and both dogs at the door waited motionless, too, until May smiled and nodded.

"Jeez, you're right," he said, as an explosion of joy went off in him. "I am."